Thomas Augustus Bland

Life of Benjamin F. Butler

Thomas Augustus Bland

Life of Benjamin F. Butler

ISBN/EAN: 9783337053994

Printed in Europe, USA, Canada, Australia, Japan

Cover: Foto ©Raphael Reischuk / pixelio.de

More available books at **www.hansebooks.com**

BENJAMIN F. BUTLER.

BY

T. A. BLAND, M.D.

BOSTON:

LEE AND SHEPARD, PUBLISHERS.

NEW YORK:

CHARLES T. DILLINGHAM.

1879.

TO

THE FRIENDS

OF

LIBERTY, EQUALITY, AND JUSTICE,

WHEREVER FOUND,

𝔗𝔥𝔦𝔰 𝔅𝔬𝔬𝔨 𝔦𝔰 𝔖𝔦𝔫𝔠𝔢𝔯𝔢𝔩𝔶 𝔍𝔫𝔰𝔠𝔯𝔦𝔟𝔢𝔡,

BY

THE AUTHOR.

INTRODUCTION.

BIOGRAPHY is the meat and marrow of history. Eliminate personality from the chronicles of a nation, and they would disappear from active society.

What to us were a history of Greece, without a record of the lives of Socrates, of Pericles, and Xenophon; of Rome, without Cæsar, Cicero, and Seneca; of England, without Shakspeare, Cromwell, and Newton; or of America, without Washington, Franklin, Lincoln, and other immortal spirits whose courage and wisdom laid the foundations of this grand Republic, and whose statesmanship and patriotism have preserved it?

The virtues are but glittering generalities, beautiful abstractions, not active forces, until incarnated in human form. Men endowed with intelligence, patriotism, integrity, philanthropy, courage, in large measure, are by that fact ordained representatives of grand ideas, accepted leaders of their fellows; and when the times are right for a bold forward march in the never-ending campaign of progress, or a vigorous assault upon the ever-existing strongholds of injustice and oppression, the masses find their leaders, and follow them to victory.

Now it is Leonidas, at the pass of Thermopylæ, holding back the myriad hosts of Persia, through the patriotic courage of three hundred men, who recognize him as the embodied hope of Spartan liberty. Again it is Tell, defying the arrogance of Gessler, in the name of the freedom-loving sons of Switzerland. Anon it is Cromwell, leading the Puritan armies to the overthrow of the Stuart dynasty in the name of justice and religion. Then it is Washington, marshalling the patriot hosts of America against the hired minions of George the Third. These men were the chosen executors of the will of God, the instruments by which he delivered his people from bondage.

The foes of liberty, justice, and equality; the Tory element in American society; the men who believe in the aristocracy of wealth, and the right of the rich to rule and rob the poor; those who hold that moneyed men and rich corporations should control the finances of the country, and that all legislation upon this important subject ought to be dictated by bankers and brokers, — these, taking advantage of the honest and unsuspecting people, while they were settling the question of negro-slavery by the sword, intrenched themselves in the strongholds of the Government. They bribed the venal and deceived the ignorant public men, to such an extent, that Congress, the Supreme Court, and the President became their slaves. They have ordained the platforms of both the Republican and Democratic parties for the past fifteen years, and dictated the policy of each succeeding administration. Under their selfish manipulation, the government has been practically subverted, and justice, the parent of liberty, is no longer a guide to the nation. The producing and enterprising classes are taxed to support a privileged class of untaxed, non-producing capitalists, as well as to sustain a large standing army whose chief excuse for existence is that it may protect the grasping and arrogant few against the possible vengeance of a plundered and oppressed people. And, while thus heavily burdened, our property is depreciated, and our debts correspondingly increased, by the deliberate action of Congress, and the Secretary of the Treasury, through the contraction of the currency. The men of enterprise are thus bankrupted, the wage-laborers brought to the verge of famine, and the farmers are rapidly sinking from the comfortable state of independent yeomen, to that of tenants at will.

The groans of the oppressed fill the air; the prayers of the poor ascend to Heaven; and the demand for justice is taking shape in the form of a new party of the people. Among the representatives of this new party, Gen. Benjamin F. Butler stands out as the great leader, — the man who, of all men in this country, combines the qualities of a leader such as is demanded by the exigencies of the times; a large brain, untiring energy, unswerving integrity, indomitable will, dauntless courage, independence of character: a man of intellectual power and executive force; a man who has convictions, and dares maintain them; a man who can be held to the support of a party only so long as it represents the principles which won his allegiance; a man who prefers

defeat in the right, to success in the wrong; a man whose
personal, political, and military record invites criticism, and
defies slander, and whose personal popularity is such as to
make his name a tower of strength among the honest masses.
It is such a man whose brilliant yet unfinished career is
briefly sketched in this volume.

CONTENTS.

LIFE OF BENJAMIN F. BUTLER.

CHAPTER I.

ANCESTRY, BIRTHPLACE, AND BOYHOOD.

IF ancestry and birth determine one's national and provincial status, Gen. Butler is a full-blooded American Yankee.

His grandfather, Zephania Butler, was a native of Connecticut, and commanded a company during the War of Independence; and the sword of this old Continental hero now hangs in the library of the general at Lowell.

His paternal grandmother, a daughter of Col. Cilley of Revolutionary memory, belonged to the distinguished New Hampshire family of that name.

His mother, Charlotte Elison, was the daughter of Richard Elison from the North of Ireland, whose ancestors settled in New Hampshire at once after the battle of the Boyne, wherein one took part. There is no question about the general's coming of patriotic fighting-stock.

Capt. John Butler of Deerfield, N.H., father of Gen. Butler, commanded a cavalry company in the war of 1812, and was with Gen. Jackson, being sent to him before the battle of New Orleans. After the war he took to the sea as a West-India trader, and died of yellow-fever on board his vessel in 1819. His fortune was chiefly in his ship and cargo, and but little of it ever reached his widow and children. Hence upon the intelligence, energy, and virtue of the mother depended the fate of the two sons, Andrew Jackson and Benjamin Franklin Butler; the latter being at the time of his father's death but five months old, he having first seen the light at Deerfield, N.H., Nov. 5, 1818. The future hero was a small, sickly, quiet, but very studious boy. He took to books naturally. His passion for study was so great that he devoured and digested all the books and pamphlets in the town. The Bible was the favorite book with his mother, and Benjamin delighted her heart by committing large portions of it to memory; but so he did the history of the Revolution, and many other favorite books, of prose and poetry.

If current legends are to be credited, his studious habits did not prevent his engaging in the active sports of boyhood. It is also stated on excellent authority, that, though small and sickly, he won many a victory over larger boys, in the bloody battles of the street and playground. He seldom or never fought on his own account, but as the champion of the weak and the timid, and especially the poor and despised urchins, so often imposed upon by cowardly and snobbish bullies.

The city of Lowell, Mass., was founded in 1821; and seven years later Mrs. Butler removed to the new manufacturing village, and opened a boarding-house, which proved so successful that she was able to aid her son to the advantages of a liberal education.

When ready for college, Benjamin set his heart on West Point Military Academy; but his mother, wishing him to become a Baptist minister, sent him to Waterville College, Maine, where he spent four years, graduating at the age of twenty, 1838.

His intellectual grasp and activity were so great that he not only mastered easily the regular lessons, but the ample college library also, leaving the institution an educated young man in the broadest and truest sense. He was a leader among the more literary students, and through his influence some important reforms were inaugurated in the college societies. His mind was of the original and independent type, and so comprehensive and clear, that he saw many defects and errors in the ideas and rules by which the college was governed, as well as in the system of theology proclaimed in the chapel. He believed that to develop and train the mind, and supply it with information upon all useful subjects, is to educate it: hence he was not willing to limit his opportunities to the curriculum of college studies.

To him the Calvinistic theology taught by the president and professors of the college was too narrow and dogmatic to deserve the name of religion; which, to him, meant practical reverence for God, through obedience to his laws.

One of the professors delivered a sermon in the chapel, in which he said, " 1. None but the elect can be saved. 2. Of so-called Christians, probably not more than one in a hundred will be saved. 3. Heathen people will have more consideration of the Almighty in future life than men of Christian nations who hear, but do not profit by the word of God."

The rules of the institution enforced attendance upon chapel-services, and after hearing this sermon young Butler petitioned the faculty to relieve him from further attendance upon preaching : giving as a reason, that, according to the proportion stated, not above six persons in the college could possibly be saved ; and as there were nine worthy professors, all of whom were doctors of divinity, it would be presumptuous for him, a poor student, to even hope for the remotest chance of salvation : hence in attending church he was only making his damnation more certain and terrible. Two or three of the faculty could appreciate the humor, if not the logic, of the petition ; and this saved the young theological reformer from expulsion for irreverence.

On leaving college, young Butler weighed but ninety-seven pounds, and gave little promise of the vigorous manhood he has since developed.

The first thing he did was just the right thing. He went to sea with an uncle of his, captain of a fishing-schooner. The cruise lasted four months, during which the young student worked hard, ate immense rations of codfish, and came back home robust and healthy. From that time to this he has enjoyed excellent health ; and his constitution is un-doubtedly one of the most vigorous and enduring to be found anywhere.

He has maintained that vigor by obedience to the laws of health, in matters of diet, exercise, &c. He is regular and temperate in his habits : hence the secret of his ability to do more brain-work than almost any other man in this country.

CHAPTER II.

HIS CAREER AS A LAWYER.

ON being thwarted in his wish to obtain a military training, young Butler wished to become a physician ; but, before leaving college, this purpose was abandoned, and on his return to Lowell, from his fishing-voyage, he entered upon the study of the law. His poverty compelled him to teach school at intervals, to meet personal expenses, until qualified to practise in the local courts. He was regarded an excellent school-teacher ; and, long before he asked for admission to the bar, he had won considerable reputation as an attorney in minor causes. His first clients were factory-girls who felt themselves wronged by oppressive corporations. At first these poor girls came to young Butler for advice because they were not able to pay regular lawyers' fees, and were sure of his sympathy and advice, whether they could pay him or not. He took their cases, and usually won them ; which fact attracted attention, and brought him other clients. Sometimes he would get two or three dollars for trying a cause : at other times his fee would consist entirely of profuse and grateful thanks.

He worked and studied about eighteen hours a day, taking no recreation save such as he found in the exercises of the military company to which he belonged, and which he joined as a private soon after he commenced the study of the law. This company was called the City Guard, and was a part of the famous Sixth Regiment of Massachusetts militia, mobbed in the streets of Baltimore on the memorable 19th of April, 1861. It is worthy of note, that Gen. Butler rose, step by step, from the rank of private to that of brigadier-general, in the militia of his State, before the war.

Mr. Butler was admitted to the bar in 1840, at the age of twenty-two, and almost immediately took a leading position in the profession, both in point of ability and business.

His well-known and active friendship for the laboring classes rendered him unpopular with the aristocracy, and especially with the mill-owners. But his great ability, and almost marvellous success in winning cases, alarmed them; and a committee, headed by the attorney for the principal corporations, waited upon him. The old attorney said, " Mr. Butler, you are a very smart young man, and, if you pursue the proper course, you are destined to achieve both fame and fortune in your profession; but it is rich corporations, and not poor factory-girls, that enable an attorney to have a large bank-account." Butler's reply was characteristic of the man. He said, " There are always two sides to a lawsuit. If I am not for you, I shall be against you; and you can take your choice."

About this time the factory-girls, to the number of three thousand, struck for a reduction in the hours of labor, a day's work being thirteen hours.

The girls appointed a committee to invite young lawyer Butler to address them in the grove. He at once accepted. He said, "Your grievances are great, your claims just, but you are not likely to bring your employers to terms by the rash measure you are taking. Your places can be readily filled, and you cannot afford to be thrown out of work. A strike is, at least, a doubtful and generally a desperate measure, and only to be resolved upon as a last resort, when oppression is no longer endurable or otherwise curable." He advised them to return to work, and try remonstrance, and, if that failed, appeal to the legislature to limit the hours of labor. The girls took the advice of their friend and advocate, and Butler received the thanks of their employers for his sensible speech. This incident served to enthuse him in favor of a law limiting a day's work to ten or eleven hours; and it was mainly due to his efforts as a member of the Legislature of the State, that the eleven-hour law was passed.

Gen. Butler possesses the qualities of a lawyer in the highest degree, — quick perception, comprehensive, and tenacious memory, a causative and logical mind, a keen sense of humor, force of character, and unswerving devotion to his clients.

He takes no case until he understands it; and then he bends all his powers to it, with faith in, and determination to win it. He believes in law; and, like Socrates, he acts on the principle, that, whether the law is good or bad, it should be executed: it is the business of the law-maker, not the attorney, to alter the statutes. He takes every advantage in favor of his client, the law gives him. There is a prevalent notion that he is a tricky lawyer. This is false, utterly false. It doubtless had its origin in the minds of small attorneys, who, failing to cope with him, grew envious, and avenged themselves by slandering him. His great success is due to his ability, profundity, energy, and pertinacity. He grasps the case in its entirety, sees its weak and its strong points; and, as the testimony develops, he analyzes it, and uses it to the best possible advantage. A strong point in his favor is found in the fact, that the courts and the members of the bar recognize his ability and profound knowledge of law to so great an extent that they yield to his opinions when not sure of their own. They fear him. The following incident, related by an old soldier in a letter to the author, illustrates this proposition. He says, —

"Some years ago I had leased a house in Boston, which proved to have a leaky roof; and the first rain-storm seriously damaged my goods, and rendered myself and family uncomfortable. I asked the landlord to repair the roof. He refused. I then refused to pay the rent until the repairs should be made. His attorney informed me that I would be sued unless I paid the rent by twelve o'clock on the following day. I was almost in despair; but my wife said, 'Go and see Gen. Butler.' I did so, finding him at his home in Lowell at nine o'clock in the evening. I said, 'General, I am an old soldier, of whom you never heard. I am in trouble, and I came to you for advice.'

It was a rainy night, and my boots were muddy; but he invited me into his parlor, and, in the most kindly manner, asked me to state my case, saying, 'If I can help you, I will.' I showed him my lease, and gave him a history of the case. He said, 'You have a good case. Don't pay a dollar until full damages are allowed, and the roof repaired.' I said, 'General, I am not able to pay you much, but I want you to be my attorney till this matter is settled.' — 'Go home. Rest easy: at twelve to-morrow keep your appointment, and tell the attorney for the landlord that your attorney advises you to stand a suit.' I said, 'How much is your fee?' — 'I don't charge you any thing.' — 'But suppose the matter comes to trial?' — 'Have no fears of that. They will settle on your terms when you tell them I have the case.' At the hour appointed, I met the attorney and the landlord. They were uncompromising, till I said, 'Well, I have made up my mind to let you sue; and my attorney assures me I shall win.' — 'Who is your attorney?' — '*Gen. Benjamin F. Butler.*' They trembled at the sound of his name; and, after a brief conference with his client, the attorney told me they would settle on my terms."

It would not be difficult to fill this volume with anecdotes similar to this.

Gen. Butler gets large fees, — of course he does, — from rich men and corporations, in important cases; but he is thus enabled to advise poor people without pay. His services command large fees, because they are of great value. In speaking of this subject, in defence of Gen. Butler against his foes during the late campaign, Wendell Phillips said, "Men say he took a large fee in the case of the Farragut award. If those interested in that award had been offered Dawes's services for five thousand dollars, or Butler's at a hundred thousand, they would have eagerly clutched at Butler's."

He adds, "There is no man in public life who does as much gratuitous work as Gen. Butler. It is rare indeed that a poor man who has a grievous wrong to be righted leaves his office without a gift of Butler's services."

Gen. Butler has long been recognized as the ablest lawyer at the bar of his own State, and one of, if not the ablest, in America: hence it is but natural that he should have grown wealthy by the legitimate pursuit of his profession. He is not only a successful attorney, but a good business-man. He has made judicious investments of his surplus earnings, chiefly in manufacturing enterprises. He owns no bond, he lends no money on interest; he is not a monopolist, but a man of enterprise, who invests his money where it benefits others as well as himself. He is liberal in his habits, as well as benevolent, but not extravagant; he is neither reckless nor niggardly, but generous, prudent, industrious, and temperate. He is exceptionally free from the secret, as well as open vices, of public men. He has the brain of a Franklin, the firmness of a Jackson, the intellectual force of a Bacon, the integrity of an Aristides, and the ripe scholarship of a Cushing.

CHAPTER III.

GEN. BUTLER'S POLITICAL RECORD BEFORE THE WAR.

GEN. BUTLER is a democrat by nature and education. His whole being rebels against, repudiates, and despises arbitrary despotism and aristocratic assumption. He believes in universal suffrage, equal rights, and just laws. He indorses unreservedly the sentiments of the Declaration of Independence, and he stands by the provisions of the Constitution. He made himself, when a boy, familiar with the history of the world. He traced the conflict of political ideas, from the time governments began to be formed, to the present age. He noted the basis of this conflict, and the slow but steady progress from absolute tyranny through limited monarchy to republicanism. He discovered that the law of evolutions applies to politics as well as to natural science. He is, therefore, a reformer, but not a revolutionist. He believes in law, not license; order, not anarchy. He thinks Jefferson a better guide than Hamilton in matters pertaining to the interpretation of the Declaration of Independence, and the questions involved in and settled by the Revolution.

History teaches him that the doctrines of the old Federalists formed the basis of the Roman republic, which proved a failure, leaving the last state of that country worse than the first; while the doctrines of Jefferson and his compatriots are substantially those upon which the Swiss republic is based; and this has stood unshaken amid surrounding despotisms for five hundred years, and still stands, a proud vindication of the principles of freedom and justice as applied to government.

The general's father was a political as well as military follower of Gen. Jackson; but he died in his son's infancy. Massachusetts was a Whig State, and Lowell overwhelmingly a Whig town: hence it is not logical, indeed, would be very absurd, to conclude that Gen. Butler allied himself to the Democratic party with a view to popularity or office, or any other personal advantage.

He has been called a demagogue; but only by those who do not know the meaning of the epithet, or, knowing it, wilfully and maliciously pervert it. His entire political career is a defence of his character against so vile a charge. He is in excellent company, however. No fact of history is more clear than this, that every great man who has practically believed in the doctrine of equal rights, and shown his faith in this doctrine by defending the rights of the poor against the oppressions of the rich, has been denounced as a demagogue; notably, in modern times, by three classes, — partisan priests, partisan editors, and partisan politicians: in other words, by

clerical, editorial, and political demagogues. It is a
common remark, that Gen. Butler is the best abused
man in America; but those who have made themselves familiar with the history of partisan politics
know that Thomas Jefferson was equally, if not more
violently, abused. The opposition clergy only denounce Butler as a demagogue, and advise the people
not to vote for him. They said Jefferson ought to
be hung to the nearest tree; and in 1804, as he was
peacefully travelling in his own carriage across the
State of New Jersey, the preachers of Trenton, by
violent denunciations, so wrought upon the passions
of the people that his carriage was mobbed, and he
narrowly escaped with his life.

Gen. Butler has been on the wrong side of some
questions; but he was honestly so, and just so soon
as convinced of his error he changed his position,
and acknowledged his error. He was wrong on the
slavery question before the war. The reason for this
error was, that he never regarded it as an abstract,
but simply as a constitutional, question.

The Constitution recognized the institution of
slavery; and he maintained, that, as the Constitution
is the supreme law of the land, its provisions must
be maintained, and all rights guaranteed by it protected. The Constitution of the United States is
the national charter; and it were treason for any
individual or state to nullify or violate its plain provisions. In this doctrine he was sustained by the
great statesmen of both the great parties, as well as
by the opinions of the fathers who framed the gov-

ernment, and ordained the Constitution. Gen. Butler's doctrine has been, and is : If constitutions or
laws are wrong, change them ; but, while they exist,
maintain them, and obey them. He believed that it
was an outrage to require factory-girls and other
operatives to work thirteen hours a day ; yet he
advised them against strikes, saying, "Change the
law."

He became a candidate for the Legislature on that
issue, and was triumphantly elected. A few days
before the election, a committee of workingmen
called at his office, to say that a notice had been
posted in all the mills, that all who voted the Butler
ticket would be discharged. Here was violation of
law and of right threatened by his opponents. Oppression was to be maintained by bull-dozing, though
this word had not been invented then. He said,
"Announce me for a speech to-morrow night." The
audience was immense, expectation on tiptoe. He
began by saying, —

"I am no revolutionist. Revolution is war, the destruction
of property, the shedding of blood. The accumulations of my
lifetime are invested in this city; and its value, its continued
existence, and the value of all property, and the peace and
safety of the whole community, depend upon the peaceful
labors of the men before me. I do not counsel revolution or
violent measures ; for I do not, *I can not*, believe that the notice
posted in the mills was authorized. Some ignorant underling
has done this with the hope of propitiating the favor of distant
masters; misjudging them, misjudging you. The owners of
the mills are surely too wise, too just, or at least too prudent, to
authorize a measure which absolutely extinguishes government,

which invites, justifies, and necessitates anarchy. For tyranny less odious than this, men of Massachusetts, our fathers cast off their allegiance to the king, and plunged into the bloody chaos of revolution; and the directors must know that the sons stand ready to do as their sires have done before them. But if it should prove true that this infamous notice *was* authorized, if men are to be deprived even of the enjoyment of the primeval curse, 'By the sweat of thy face shalt thou eat thy bread,' for exercising the right of an American citizen to vote as their conciences dictate, then, WOE TO LOWELL! The place that knows it now shall know it no more forever! To my own house, I, with this hand, will first apply the torch. All I have I consecrate to the flames."

The effect of this speech was magical. The audience were so stirred, that for a few moments it seemed that nothing could prevent the burning of the city at once. But they were in the hands of a master in whom they trusted; and when he closed by saying, "My friends, go home, obey the laws, do no act of violence; and, when election-day comes, vote as your judgment shall dictate, without regard to personal consequences. Wait till overt acts of treason to liberty and law shall come from the other side." The notice disappeared at once, and Butler was elected. He has served two sessions in the House, one in the Senate, and was also a member of the State Constitutional Convention; and his record is that of a sound statesman and honest reformer.

Gen. Butler ran for governor of Massachusetts twice before the war, receiving the first time fifty thousand votes, but the other time only six thousand.

This was in 1860; and the reason for his small vote was, that he opposed the nomination first, and afterwards the election, of Douglas to the presidency. The general took such interest in politics, that he always attended the national conventions of his party; beginning with the convention of 1844, which nominated Polk for the presidency. He was sometimes on the platform committee: hence his hand and head had much to do with shaping the national policy of the party. He believed that the perpetuation of the Union, and the protection of the people's rights, depended upon the continued dominance of the Democratic party. He recognized the fact that the Whig party was the legitimate child and successor of the old Federalist party, inheriting the aristocratic ideas of Alexander Hamilton and John Adams: hence he could not regard it as a safe custodian of the rights and interests of the toiling masses. He saw also that the constitutional guaranties of the slave States were not respected by that party, as a party; and he held it sound doctrine, that, so long as the slaveholders had rights under the Constitution, those rights should be respected.

James Parton, in his book entitled "Gen. Butler in New Orleans," says, "The basis of Gen. Butler's interest in politics is an entire and fond belief in the principles upon which this government was founded, and an intense desire that the great experiment should gloriously succeed. Among educated Americans there are two kinds of men, democrats and snobs. Gen. Butler is a democrat. In the very

strength of his attachment to democratic principles
is to be found the cause of his having ignored the
rights of the negroes for so long a time. He
thought any question of their rights was. petty in
comparison with the mighty stake of mankind in the
union of these States, and the triumph of democratic institutions. The only danger to the Union,
he thought, arose from the agitation of questions
respecting slavery ; and he and his colleagues strove
with all their might to avert or defer it." He adds,
"In his speeches on the slavery question there is
candor, force, and truth ; and their argument is unanswerable if it be granted that slavery can have any
rights. There is nothing in them of base subser-
viency, nothing of insincerity, no vote-catching
vagueness." Gen. Butler was not a friend of slavery,
but of the Union and the Constitution. He had no
sympathy with the violent methods adopted by the
slaveholders to suppress free speech and crush opposition. He condemned all such measures as undem-
ocratic. He denounced the assault of Brooks upon
Sumner, in the public places of Washington, in language strong and unmistakable; and he was one of
the first to call upon the stricken senator, to assure
him of his sympathy for his sufferings and his indig-
nation at the dastardly act.

When the news of the John Brown raid on Har-
per's Ferry reached Lowell, a public meeting was
held, and Gen. Butler invited to address it. The following extract from that speech shows the spirit of the
man, and indicates clearly his position at that time : —

"It is well for us to be assembled here. Let us proclaim to all men, that the Union, first and fairest of all the good gifts of God, must and shall be preserved. That it is a duty we recognize, and will fulfil, to grant to every part of this country its rights as guaranteed by the Constitution, and due by the compact; that we will, and every part of the country shall, respect those institutions of any other part of the country with which they and we have nothing to do, save to let them alone, whether they are palatable to us, or not. . . . Thus doing our duty, and claiming our rights, and granting those of others, as any man will do who is a just man, must not the Union be perpetual? Let no man mistake upon the matter. This Union, this Republic, the great experiment of equal rights, this power of self-government by the people, this great instrument of civilization, the banding together of the intellectual and political power of those races which are to civilize the world by their energy of action, is not to fail, and human progress be set back a thousand years, because of the difference of opinion as to the supposed rights and interests of a few negroes. This Union is not like a family, because its members must never separate, and divide the homestead. It is not like a partnership, because it contains no elements or periods of dissolution. It is not like a confederation, because it contains no clause or means by which one or more of its members can withdraw. It is either organization or chaos. It may crumble into atoms: it cannot be split in fragments. A despotism may arise upon its ruins, but little snarling republics can never be made from its pieces. . . . To us no star in our glorious banner differeth from another star in glory; but all must and shall shine on together in one constellation, to bless the world with its benign radiance forever."

Are these the words of a demagogue, or the sentiments of a statesman? the rantings of a fanatic, or the calm wisdom of a philosopher? Gen. Butler attended the Charleston Convention in April, 1860, with a fixed determination to make no concessions to the South beyond those contained in the Cincinnati platform of 1856; and as a member of the Committee on Resolutions he proposed the following : —

"*Resolved*, That we, the Democracy of the Union, in convention assembled, hereby declare our affirmance of the Democratic resolutions unanimously adopted and declared as a platform of principles at Cincinnati, in the year 1856, without addition or alteration; believing that Democratic principles are unchangeable in their nature when applied to the same subject-matter."

This resolution was lost by one vote, — sixteen States for, and seventeen against it. Gen. Butler earnestly desired that the convention should harmonize upon a platform and a candidate; but, beyond the Cincinnati platform, he could offer nothing to the South. He became disgusted with Douglas, or rather with his friends who represented him in the convention, because he saw a disposition to offer more than the South asked. They were willing to concede any thing for the sake of the nomination of the Little Giant of squatter sovereignty. But the representative men of the party, and especially of the South, were averse to Judge Douglas; they distrusted him, and their distrust increased in proportion to the overtures made by the Douglas delegates.

There were three platforms reported to the convention; one from the majority, one from the minority, of the committee, and one from Gen. Butler, who had refused to indorse the report of either faction of the committee, but stood by the Cincinnati platform. He made a speech in favor of his report and in opposition to the objectionable features of the others.   He said, —

"If the Cincinnati platform is so defective, why did you give it such enthusiastic support in 1856?   I am told that it is capable of two interpretations.   Why, sir, when Omniscience sends us a divine law for our guidance through life, and our hope in death, for almost two thousand years men have been engaged in giving different interpretations of that law, and they have sealed their faith in their own interpretations with their blood. They have burned each other at the stake as an evidence of the sincerity of their faith."

Speaking of the majority report, he said, —

"Our opponents will see in it, what I hope Southern gentlemen do not mean, — the re-opening of the African slave-trade; and it will be so construed that no man can get rid of the interpretation.   It will be proclaimed from every stump, flaunted from every pulpit, thundered from every platform, in the North, until we, your friends, — and in no boasting spirit I say, without us you are powerless, — the last refuge of the constitutional rights of the South, are stricken down powerless forever; so that without modification it would be impossible for me to adopt the report."

He proceeded to review the resolutions presented by the Douglas wing of the committee, showing how weak and silly they were, — a mere web of sophistry to catch gulls.   He punctured the carefully worded resolutions.

"Leaving the whole matter of slavery in either States or territories to the Supreme Court, suppose, gentlemen of the North, the Supreme Court should decide that slavery exists in Massachusetts, that it was forced upon us by the Constitution of the United States: what would you do about it?

"And you, gentlemen of the South, suppose in the course

of a few years the Supreme Court should become anti-slavery, and make a decision that slavery nowhere exists by natural law and that men can hold no property in man: what then? Are you prepared to abide by the decision?"

At this point a delegate from Maryland, Mr. Johnson, interrupted him by saying that it became a man representing a State that never gave a Democratic majority, to be modest about offering advice to a Democratic convention. Gen. Butler is most happy at retort, and he was ready now: —

"You may taunt me with the fact that I am speaking for poor old Massachusetts, who has not given a Democratic vote since the days of Jefferson: she did give a Democratic vote *then*. By that vote the South acquired the rich inheritance of Louisiana; and I see here from the Gulf States men whom but for that vote I never would have had the pleasure of meeting, except as subjects of Napoleon III.

"Then do not taunt me with speaking for a State that cannot give an electoral vote. I feel bad enough about it. I do not like to be taunted with it. I think it especially unkind of my friend from Maryland, because he violated the well-known maxim, that the pot should never call the kettle black."

Mr. Johnson replied, "While Maryland obeys the laws of the Union, as she has ever done, she considers herself equal to all other States; but, when she refuses to acknowledge the force of the Constitution, she will then be more modest in the expression of her opinions."

"Comparisons are odious," responded Gen. Butler; "but I say that any man in Massachusetts can walk up to the polls, and vote as he pleases, without danger of having his head broken by a club."

Gen. Butler's report was adopted by a large majority of the convention, 230 to 40.   The next thing was to nominate a candidate to stand upon it.   The result is a matter of history.

Gen. Butler, in his report to his constituents on his return from the convention, says, —

"With the facts before me, and impressing upon me the conviction that the nomination of Judge Douglas could not be made with any hope of safety to the Democratic party, what was I to do? Yielding to your preferences, I voted seven times for Judge Douglas, although my judgment told me that my votes were worse than useless, as they gave him an appearance of strength in the convention which I felt he had not in the party.

"I then looked about me, with a view to throwing my vote where, at least, it would not mislead any one. I saw a statesman of national fame, who had led his regiment to victory at Buena Vista, a Democrat with whom I disagreed in some things, but with whom I could act in most, — loving his country first, his section next, but just to all, so that, through his endeavors in the Senate of the United States, Massachusetts obtained from the General Government several hundred thousand dollars, her just dues deferred for forty years, — a feat which none of her own sons had ever been able to accomplish. Besides, his friends were not pressing his name before the convention, so that he was not a party to the personal strife then going on. I thought such a man worthy of the poor compliment of a vote from Massachusetts: therefore I threw my vote for Jefferson Davis of Mississippi. I make no apology for that vote. I believe it was guided by an intelligent view of the situation."

After fifty-seven ballotings, without a nomination, the convention adjourned, to meet in Baltimore on the 18th of June.

There Judge Douglas's friends maintained their fixed determination to force him upon the party, and the convention again split. Gen. Butler, being unalterably opposed to the nomination of Douglas, went with the delegates who agreed with him in this opposition.

The Douglas men nominated their favorite, with Herschel V. Johnson of Georgia, an avowed disunionist, for the second office. The other party nominated Breckenridge of Kentucky for the presidency, and Lane of Oregon for vice-president.

In justice to Gen. Butler, let it be stated that his candidate stood upon a platform which left the people of each territory free to form a constitution, and come into the Union, as a slave State or as a free State.

The platform of Douglas said, "The Supreme Court shall decide the matter, both for the States and Territories; and its decisions shall be final."

The Republican platform, upon which Mr. Lincoln was placed, said, "There is no authority anywhere which can sustain slavery in the territories of this country. Neither Congress nor the Supreme Court can do it." If Gen. Butler was wrong, it was certainly not in his decision between the two Democratic platforms. He was wiser than a majority of his party at that time. He demonstrated his honesty by opposing the sophistical demagoguery of the Douglas faction. I do not hesitate to say that from a Democratic standpoint he acted right; and it is a source of satisfaction to the writer, that, as a Republican, he said so publicly during that ever memorable campaign.

In a speech in Lowell, in defence of his position, Gen. Butler said, —

"We who support Mr. Breckenridge are called disunionists. By whom is this charge made? By Pierre Soulé of Louisiana, an avowed disunionist; by John Forsythe; and the Atlanta Confederacy, which maintains the duty of the South to leave the Union if Lincoln is elected. And yet these men are the foremost in promoting the election of Douglas. By Goulding of Georgia, who is making the same speech in the campaign for Douglas that he made in the Baltimore convention, where he argued that non-intervention meant that Congress had no power to prevent the exportation of negroes from Africa, and that popular sovereignty meant the re-establishment of the slave-trade. When I left that convention, I declared that I would no longer sit where the African slave-trade, made piracy and felony by the laws of my country, was openly advocated and applauded. Yet such at the South are the supporters of Douglas."

Gen. Butler knew that quite a considerable number of Southern leaders were ready to favor secession in the event of the election of Lincoln; but he did not believe that a majority of them would sustain so rash and treasonable a measure. An agreement had been made at Baltimore, that if Lincoln should be chosen, — which was then thought probable, — the Democratic leaders should meet in Washington on the 1st of December, 1860, to consult together on the situation. Accordingly Gen. Butler repaired to the capital on the opening of Congress, where he met quite a large number of his party friends. South

Carolina had already seceded, and sent three men, commissioned to act for the State in negotiating terms of separation. To the headquarters of this trio of traitors, the general repaired. He found a large number of representative Southerners there, who, to his surprise, talked as though they regarded a dissolution of the Union a settled fact. Among the few who opposed this view of the situation, Mr. Breckenridge stood out prominent. The brilliant ex-candidate joined Gen. Butler in an earnest effort to stay the tide of treason, and save the old party, the South, and the Union. They met with very little encouragement, little sympathy even.

"What does this mean?" asked Butler of a prominent Southern Democrat, soon after his arrival.

"It means simply what it appears to mean. The Union is dead. The experiment is finished. The attempt of two communities having no interest in common, to live together, to make believe they are one nation, has ceased forever. We shall establish a sound, homogeneous government, with no discordant elements. We shall have room for our friends. Come with us."

"Have you counted the cost? Do you really think you can break up this Union? Do *you* think so, yourself?"

"I do."

"You are, then, prepared for civil war? You mean to bring this matter to the issue of arms?"

"Oh, the North won't fight!"

"The North *will* fight."

"The North can't fight. We have friends enough at the North to prevent it."

"You have friends at the North as long as you remain true to the Constitution and the Union. But, the moment it is seen that you mean to break up the nation, that moment the North is a unit against you. I can answer for Massachusetts. She is good for ten thousand men to march at once against armed Secession."

"Massachusetts is not such a fool. If your State should attempt to send an army to preserve the Union, she would have to fight twice as large an army at home, who will oppose such a policy."

"No, sir: when we come from Massachusetts to fight for the Union, we shall not leave a single traitor behind, unless we leave him hanging on a tree. I know something of the North, and a good deal about New England. We are pretty quiet there now, because we don't believe you mean to carry out your threats. But, as sure as you attempt to break up this Union, the North will resist the attempt, to the last man and the last dollar; and you are as certain to fail as there is a God in heaven. You may ruin the South, and blot out slavery; but you can't destroy the Union. God and nature, and the blood of your fathers and mine, have made it one; and one it must remain forever."

"Would you fight against us?"

"I would; and, by the grace of God, *I will.*"

Gen. Butler called on the President, Buchanan, and Attorney-General Black, to present his plan for crushing treason while yet in the bud. He said, "Secession is treason; and the presenting of an ordinance of secession is an overt act of treason. These so-called commissioners from South Carolina are coming to the White House to present the ordinance to the President. Admit them. Let them present the ordinance. Have a United-States marshal present, with orders to arrest them as prisoners of state, charged with treason. Try them before the Supreme Court, as we did Aaron Burr. I will stay here, and help the district attorney, without fee or reward. If they are convicted, hang them, if that is the sentence. If they are acquitted, you will have done something toward leaving a clear path for the incoming administration. Time will have been gained; for both sides will pause, and watch the dignified proceedings. Passions will cool, the points at issue will become clear to all parties; and, in my opinion, the threatened storm will pass by."

The Attorney-General favored Gen. Butler's plan, but the President refused to sanction it. Thus, through the weakness and timidity of one man, who held supreme power, was the scheme of the ablest and most daring of American statesmen rejected, — a scheme which few can doubt was wisely planned, and would have been successful.

Gen. Butler had many long and earnest interviews with the Southern leaders, during which he used every art of argument and persuasion of which he was master, with the hope of changing their purpose; but all was vain. They adhered to their purpose,

and urged him to join them, offering every induce-
ment in the form of office, honors, money. But he
checked them by saying, "I pardon the insult you
offer me, that we may to-night part as friends ; but,
unless you repent of your rash purpose, we meet no
more, except, perchance, on the battle-field, as mortal
foes."

He at once called on his old friend Senator Wil-
son of Massachusetts, to lay before him all the facts
he had gathered, and ask him to join him in a letter
to the governor of their State, suggesting the importance of putting the militia of the Commonwealth on
a war footing at once, with a view to possible emer-
gency. On his return to Boston he had a personal
interview with Gov. Andrew. The result was the
adoption of his advice. The governor could hardly
believe the danger so imminent as Gen. Butler represented it ; but the stirring events of the next few
months fully sustained the wisdom of his opinion
and counsel.

CHAPTER IV.

GEN. BUTLER'S RECORD AS A SOLDIER.

THE booming of rebel cannon fired on Fort Sumter awoke not only the echoes of Charleston Harbor, but the slumbering patriotism of a nation of freemen.

On the 15th of April, 1861, Gen. Butler was engaged upon a case in a Boston court. The hand on the dial of time pointed to a quarter to five, P.M., when Col. Jones of the Sixth Regiment of Massachusetts militia entered, and handed the general an order from the governor of the State, to muster his command forthwith on Boston Common. To read and indorse this order, was the work of a moment; and the brave colonel started for Lowell to call his men together. The general handed his briefs to an associate attorney, and followed on the 5.30 train.

At eleven o'clock on the morning of the 16th, the regiment, the colonel, and the general were on Boston Common awaiting orders, though it had cost a whole night of active effort to collect the various companies from their different and widely separated homes. The first requisition of the Secretary of War had been for two regiments to defend Washington. On this day he telegraphed for a brigade of four full regiments, and a brigadier-general to command it. Gen. Pierce was the ranking brigadier in the State, and a political as well as personal friend of the governor; yet the command was tendered to Gen. Butler, who at once accepted it. It was decided to send the Sixth forward at once; and it left at four that afternoon, after hearing stirring words of patriotic cheer from Gov. Andrew and Gen. Butler. At midnight the general went to his home, awoke his family from their peaceful slumbers, only to embrace his wife and children, and bid them good-by. An early train from Lowell bore him to Boston in company with his brother Andrew J., then on a visit to his early home from California, and who accepted a position on the staff of the general.

Two regiments were sent by steamer to Fortress Monroe; but the Eighth, with Gen. Butler in immediate command, took the train for Washington *via* New York and Philadelphia. In New York they were entertained at the Astor and Metropolitan hotels; and on arriving at Philadelphia they were quartered at the Girard, and generously fed by the citizens of the city. Here the news of the attack on the Sixth Regiment by the Baltimore mob reached the general. He also learned that the bridges were on fire: hence it would be impossible to reach Washington *via* Baltimore. The general consulted the map, and resolved to go to Havre de Grace by rail, thence to Annapolis by steamer, and from there to Washington by railroad. Rumor said, "Maryland is full of armed rebels, and hard fighting may be expected;" but Gen. Butler had started for Washington under orders, and he meant to get there at the earliest possible moment. His plans were determined upon; and then he called his officers together, and laid them before them, saying, "I take the responsibility upon myself, and now invite you to share the dangers." Not a man faltered. Sketching his plans to be forwarded to Gov. Andrew after his departure, he started with his regiment for Havre de Grace. Col. Lefferts of the Seventh New York was there with his regiment, and was asked by the general to go with him; but, regarding the peril too great, he declined.

Arriving at Havre de Grace, the general took possession of the steam ferry-boat, and, embarking with his command, ordered the captain to steer for Annapolis by the shortest route. The general had doubts as to the loyalty of the captain and crew of the steamer "Maryland:" hence he kept watch personally while his men slept.

They hove in sight of the capital of Maryland at midnight, and were surprised to find the city illuminated. Ordering the anchor overboard, he sent his brother in a small boat, to learn why the people were so wide awake. Col. Butler landed at the Naval Academy, and had an interview with Capt. Blake, commandant of the post. Scarcely had Col. Butler reached the shore, when a boat was seen approaching the steamer, and a voice called out, "What steamer is this?"

Receiving no reply, the boat was making for the shore when Gen. Butler called out, "Come on board, or I will fire into you."

This boat proved to have been sent by Capt. Blake, to ascertain the name and object of the steamer. Lieut. Matthews and Gen. Butler soon came to an understanding, and were mutually delighted, being both true patriots. Capt. Blake, though loyal, advised the general not to land; and Gov. Hicks forbade his doing so, in a written order.

He disregarded both the captain's advice and the governor's order. Before landing, however, he towed the old school-ship "Constitution," which lay at the wharf aground, in imminent danger of capture by the rebels, out to sea, thus saving her to the Government. Gen. Butler was informed that it would be impossible to reach Washington, as the railroad had been destroyed, and the woods were full of armed rebels; and, still worse, that not a citizen of Annapolis would give or sell him any thing for him or his soldiers to eat.

The general replied to this last terrible news, that he had hoped for more hospitable treatment, but that his soldiers were not apt to suffer for food: if ordinary means did not suffice to procure it, there were measures known to soldiers that would not fail. The hint was sufficient. The soldiers found no difficulty in purchasing supplies. In the mean time Col. Lefferts with his Seventh New York arrived; he having been compelled to adopt Gen. Butler's route to Washington, after he had left Philadelphia. The two regi-

ments greeted each other with hearty cheers, and
fraternized at once; but, on hearing the cock-and-bull
stories with which Gov. Hicks and the citizens of
Annapolis had tried in vain to frighten Gen. Butler,
Col. Lefferts declined the second time to join the general in his march to the capital, resolving to remain
in the fort until re-enforcements should arrive. Parton says, "Vain were arguments; vain remonstrance;
vain the biting taunt. Col. Lefferts still refused to
go." Gen. Butler said, "Then we go alone." He
seized the railroad depot and storehouse, forcing the
gates. Finding an old locomotive, he put it in
charge of Charles Homans, a private of Company
E, a locomotive-builder by trade, who soon had it in
working trim. The railroad-track had been torn up;
but there were plenty of men in his regiment who
knew how to build railroads, and these were set to
work. At dawn of the next day all was in readiness
for a start to Washington; and Col. Lefferts having
got over his scare, and his men and officers being
anxious to share the dangers and glory of the bold
march, relented, and, to Gen. Butler's delight, announced his purpose to go with him.

The general took every precaution against successful attack, by mounting loaded howitzers on platform
cars, and ordering his men to keep their arms in
hand ready for momentary use in case of attack.
Thus this indomitable soldier forwarded his command through a hostile country to the capital of the
nation, laying track and building bridges as they
went. His fearless courage overawed his foes, and

no attack was made upon his little army of Spartan Yankees.

After getting the two regiments well on their way, and assuring himself of their entire safety, he returned to Annapolis, under orders from Gen. Scott, who created the Department of Annapolis, the command of which he assigned to Brig.-Gen. Benjamin F. Butler. His instructions gave him almost absolute power; and this power he never abused, but used it wisely and well. Large bodies of troops landed here, and were forwarded by Gen. Butler on to Washington. He established a system of strict surveillance over travel between the North and South, arresting all spies and suspicious characters, giving passports only to those who could show a clear record. He kept a strict watch on the governor and legislature of Maryland; and, having got possession of the seal of the State, he prevented the passage, or rather the legalizing, of any act of treason.

His great services were highly appreciated by President Lincoln, as well as by Gen. Scott and the Secretary of War; and the governor and people of Massachusetts felt justly proud of their distinguished citizen-general.

Gen. Butler was always a Democrat with anti-slavery proclivities; but he believed in carrying out that, and all other reforms, within the Democratic party. For he looked to disruption of the Union when it should be attempted to be done by legal enactment; because he held, as a lawyer, that the Constitution gave the right to that species of property to the South. He was very active in the election of Mr. Sumner, in forming a coalition between the Demo-cratic party and the Free-soil party in Massachusetts, by the united votes of which Charles Sumner was elected to the United States Senate. And, foresee-ing what actually happened, the worst that could be said of him in that regard is, that he, like Lincoln, preferred the union of the States and the integrity of the Government, with slavery, rather than the disrup-tion of the country, and the breaking of the Republic into fragments, and that a portion of it should not have slavery.

When the South, by the Rebellion, broke all con-stitutional obligations, he held that they gave up all constitutional rights, and that he was set free in that regard from all constitutional restrictions; and, from that hour, gave to his anti-slavery predilections free scope, looking upon the necessary and actual result of the war, which he had done his best to stave off, to be the entire abolition of that institution.

CHAPTER V.

THE CAPTURE OF BALTIMORE.

THE first regiment to march to the defence of the Union, under the call of President Lincoln, was the Sixth Massachusetts, the regiment in which Gen. Butler had enlisted as a private at the age of twenty-two ; the regiment in which he had served as a private soldier, corporal, sergeant, second lieutenant, first lieutenant, captain, major, lieutenant-colonel, and colonel, and which formed a part of his brigade at the beginning of the war. This regiment was fired upon by a mob of rebel citizens while quietly marching through the streets of Baltimore, on the 19th of April, 1861. This regiment furnished the first victims immolated upon the altar of freedom at the opening of the new dispensation, — the first blood that crimsoned anew the glorious flag, twice baptized in the rich life-currents that flowed from the loyal hearts of our patriot fathers. Baltimore was still dominated by that murderous mob of traitors, though the majority of her citizens were loyal and true. This was enough to fill the heart of Gen. Butler with a burning desire to go to Balti-

more.   But this was not all: Baltimore was the gateway between the North and the South; and the key
was in the hands of the rebels, who were thus able,
in large measure, to prevent communication between
the capital and the loyal part of the nation.

Northern journals and the Northern people were
demanding of the War Office the subjugation of
Baltimore, and re-opening of the gateway to Washington.

Gen. Scott at length saw the necessity of it, and
formulated a plan, which he presented to Gens.
Butler, Patterson, and others.   This plan involved
the necessity of an army of twelve thousand men,
in four grand divisions, to march simultaneously to
the attack of Baltimore, and another army of ten
thousand to guard Washington, and act as a reserve.

Gen. Butler had a plan which he presented, but
which the once grand but now superannuated hero of
Lundy's Lane rejected promptly; which rejection the
War Department subsequently pronounced the greatest mistake of the ever memorable campaign of 1861.

This plan comprehended as its chief feature the
occupation and fortification of Manassas Junction,
and the cutting-off of all railway connection between
the South and Washington.   This would have saved
us the disaster and disgrace of the battle of Bull
Run.

To take possession of and occupy Baltimore was
another important part of his programme.   To this
Gen. Scott listened with some patience; but he did
not believe it could be effected without a large army,

and in his opinion it would require considerable time.

Gen. Butler succeeded in obtaining permission to change his base of operations from Annapolis to the Relay House, situated nine miles west of Baltimore; and being informed, that, as a department commander, he was wholly unrestricted save in regard to matters covered by positive orders from Washington, he resolved upon capturing Baltimore upon his own hook, and thus surprise both the rebels and his chief. Little thought he that Gen. Scott would be as indignant at such a bold *coup d'état* as the worst Baltimore plug-ugly could be.

On the 6th of May, Gen. Butler reached the Relay House with the Sixth Massachusetts, Eighth New York, and Cook's battery. He cultivated and encouraged friendly relations with the citizens of the village and vicinity; but he arrested every man who gave utterance to rebel sentiments in his camp. A Baltimore man spoke approvingly of the action of the mob, which attacked the Sixth Massachusetts, in the presence of some of the soldiers, who at once arrested him; and by order of the general he was sent to Annapolis a prisoner.

Baltimore was in Gen. Butler's department, of which fact he reminded Gen. Scott by special despatch on the 13th of May. The reply assured him that Gen. Scott was glad Baltimore was in his department, and desired to invite his special attention to the fact, that, according to information deemed reliable, there was a large amount of powder

stored in a church in that city, which he feared might
fall into active rebel hands, and be used against the
Government. The same day, in the afternoon, Gen.
Butler left Relay on two trains, going toward Har-
per's Ferry. The smaller train, with some fifty men,
was bound for Frederick City to capture Ross Winans, the millionnaire, traitor, and inventor of the
Winans steam-gun. The other, with its nine hundred men, two field-pieces, Gen. Butler and his staff,
with their horses, was really bound for Baltimore ;
but, as there were probably spies constantly watch-
ing his movements, the general adopted that ruse to
throw them off the right scent. After running a few
miles, the engine of the longer train was reversed
and it backed down to Baltimore, passing the Relay
House without stopping, arriving in the city about
half-past seven, in the midst of a furious storm.
The general describes this storm as the most terrific
he ever witnessed. This had served to drive the
people indoors,.and he led his troops from the Cam-
den-street depot to Federal Hill without attracting
scarcely any attention. He had given orders for a
quiet march without music or conversation ; but, if
fired upon, the house from whence the shot came was
to be demolished, and the inmates arrested. No
such enlivening incident occurred. The little army
reached the summit of Federal Hill in safety, and,
planting their field-pieces, were in possession of
the city without loss of a charge of powder. The
soldiers pitched their tents, the quartermaster
brought a lot of wood from the nearest yard ; and

soon all fatigue was forgotten in a royal supper of fat pork, hard-tack, and hot coffee. The *réveille* on Federal Hill gave the city an early awakening and a wonderful surprise. They could scarcely believe that those blue-coated forms on the hill were real live Yankees. They were half inclined to the opinion that they were apparitions, or phantoms of their disordered imaginations. But at nine, A.M., a late edition of "The Clipper" gave them Gen. Butler's proclamation. It was dated, "Department of Annapolis, Federal Hill, Baltimore, May 14, 1861." It gave the citizens to clearly understand that he had taken possession of the city for the purpose of maintaining order, and enforcing obedience to law ; that no loyal, peaceably-disposed person would be disturbed ; that private property would be respected, &c.

He invited the co-operation of the civil authorities of the city in maintaining order, and in every way assured them that he regarded the city as loyal to the government of the United States. No resistance was attempted, no disturbance, worthy of mention occurred. But before the close of the memorable 14th of May, something occurred to disturb Gen. Butler. It was the following telegram from Washington : —

"SIR, — Your hazardous occupation of Baltimore was made without my knowledge, and, of course, without my approbation. It is a godsend that it was without conflict of arms."

This furious telegram bore the name of the three-hundred-pound thunderer, Lieut.-Gen. Winfield Scott.

Gen. Butler had overworked, and was really ill; and this was a heavy dose of bad medicine. He had accomplished in a few days, with less than one thousand soldiers, and without the loss of a man, what Gen. Scott proposed to do in three months, with twelve thousand men. True, he had incurred some risk; but, as Parton puts it, " Being only a volunteer general, and not a West Point graduate, he did not understand how war was to be carried on without incurring some risk of a conflict with the enemy now and then."

Gen. Scott was furious at the audacity of Gen. Butler, and nothing would appease his wrath but his immediate recall. So Butler was ordered to report at Washington, to receive a violent reproof from Gen. Scott, and a profusion of high compliments and grateful thanks from Secretary Cameron and President Lincoln.

CHAPTER VI.

GEN. BUTLER IS PROMOTED TO MAJOR-GENERAL, AND PUT IN COMMAND OF FORTRESS MONROE.

PRESIDENT LINCOLN not only congratulated Gen. Butler on his brilliant success in taking Baltimore, but he tendered him a commission as major-general, as a substantial proof of his appreciation of his ability and services, saying, "Now, general, take your old command, and go down to Fortress Monroe. Whatever additional force you may ask for, shall be furnished you, with a view to the ultimate capture of Norfolk." Parton says, "Gens. McClellan and Banks were still in the pay of their respective railroad companies when Gen. Butler received his promotion: hence he was the senior major-general in the service of the United States."

He reached Fortress Monroe on the morning of May 22. He found that almost every thing needful for comfort, use, and success, was wanting, except soldiers; and these he had brought with him. The old fort was dilapidated, and at best incapable of furnishing quarters for his force. There were no horses nor wagons, and the water was a mile away, the wood nearly as far ; and all supplies of provisions had to be carried on the backs of the soldiers, or rolled in barrels, by hand, on the ground, from the wharf to the fort.

The general began to ask for what was imperiously demanded, and he at once began not to get it. He then got permission for his brother to purchase a lot of horses. He got the permission, but not the horses ; for, just as they were ready to ship, a requisition from the War Department took them out of Col. Butler's hands, and put them in the artillery-service at Washington. This is a fair sample of the treatment he received : hence it were useless to particularize. He did not permit his embarrassments to cool his ardor, or lessen his active efforts to do good service. He reconnoitred the surrounding country. He occupied Newport News, with the ultimate view of capturing Richmond, and ending the rebellion.

THE FIRST CONTRABANDS.

On the evening of May 24, 1861, Major-Gen. Butler was informed that three negro men had been brought into camp at their own request, they having voluntarily surrendered to one of his pickets. These negroes said they had belonged to Col. Mallory, who was on the point of sending them to North Carolina to work on rebel forts ; and they objected to being separated from their families. Gen. Butler reflected a moment. Here was a great question to be solved.

Col. Mallory was a rebel; and if his horses, or any ordinary property belonging to him, had fallen into Gen. Butler's hands, he would not have hesitated about using it in the service of the country. Then why not his slaves?

These negroes were about to be set to work on rebel fortifications, to be utilized against the Government: they were regarded as property by their masters; and, if so, why not, like other property, subject to confiscation?

"The South," said Wendell Phillips, "fought to sustain slavery, and the North fought not to have it hurt." Here was a conundrum; and Gen. Butler solved it by pronouncing that magical word, "*contraband*." Yes, these negroes are, according to the rules of war, contraband; and he ordered them set to work.

The news spread among the slave-population, and the negroes came in from every quarter daily.

A rebel officer, Major Carey, sent Gen. Butler a note asking an interview on the high road, a mile from the fort. It was granted at once; and the general, accompanied by his staff, rode out to meet some of his old Democratic friends, whom he had not seen since the adjournment of the Baltimore Convention. After a polite but rather stately greeting, Major Carey said, —

"I wish to know, sir, upon what principles you propose to conduct the war? I am agent for Col. Mallory; and, having learned that three negroes belonging to him have escaped within your lines, I wish to ask what you mean to do with them?"

"I propose to keep them, and make them useful to the Government."

"Do you mean, then, to set aside your constitutional obligations?"

"I mean to abide by the decision of Virginia, as expressed in her ordinance of secession passed day before yesterday. I am under no constitutional obligations to a foreign country, which Virginia now claims to be."

"But you say we can't secede, and so you can't consistently detain the negroes."

"But you say you have seceded: hence you can't consistently claim them. I shall hold them as contraband of war. You were using them against the Government: I propose to use them in favor of it. If, however, Col. Mallory will come in and take the oath of allegiance to the United States, he shall have his negroes."

At this point the conversation ended.

Gen. Butler wrote the Government in regard to this matter, giving his views very fully. He said, among other things, "These negroes are being used against the Government by its foes. They were used in the erection of Sewell's-Point batteries, from which my command was fired on. Without them these batteries could not have been built for many weeks, at least. As a military question, it would seem to be a matter of necessity to deprive the rebels of their services; and, if I accept the services of father and mother, would not sentiments of humanity dictate that I also take care of the children?"

The Secretary of War wrote, in reply, that his conduct in regard to the negroes was fully approved by the Government.   But the slaveholding rebel authorities, and the kid-gloved West-Point *dilettanti*, condemned it.   In the light of gathered experience, who does not pronounce it one of the wisest, grandest, and most patriotic measures of that stormy but wonderfully educative era?

Many incidents of interest occurred in this connection; some amusing, others pathetic, some combining the two.   The following will serve as an illustration of the latter class.   An old Virginia gentleman came to Gen. Butler's headquarters one day, to ask that one of his thirty negroes, who had all escaped to the fort, might be returned.

His countenance was elongated by sadness, and clouded by grief; and his voice quavered as though partially paralyzed by a touch from the wand of despair.   He said, "I allers treated my niggers kind, and I thought they all loved me.   Last Sunday I went to the house of God; and, when I got back, I entered my house, and I found nobody there.   I called for Mary, to take off my coat, and hang it up; but Mary didn't come.   Then I went into the next room, to find Mary; but I found her not: there was no Mary there.   I went into the kitchen; but there was nobody in the kitchen.   I went into the garden; but there was nobody in the garden.   I went to the nigger-quarters; but there was nobody in the nigger-quarters.   I went into my house, and I felt very lonesome.   After a while Jeems came to me.   Jeems

is my body-sarvant, and he has sarved me faithfully
for many years.

"I asked Jeems what had happened, and Jeems
said all the people had gone to the fort.

"'While I was at the house of God, Jeems?'

"'Yes, massa: they're all-gone.'

"And I said to Jeems, 'Why didn't you go too,
Jeems?'

"And Jeems said, 'Oh, massa! I'll never leave
you.'

"'Well, Jeems,' said I, 'as there's nobody to cook,
see if you can't get me some cold vittles and some
whiskey, Jeems.'

"And, when I had eaten, I said to Jeems, —

"'Jeems, it's no use our stayin' here. We will go
to your mistress.' His mistress, sir, had gone away
from home about eleven miles, fleeing from the
dangers of the war. And so, 'Jeems,' said I, 'har-
ness up the best horse to the cart, and put into the
cart our best bed, and some bacon, and some corn-
meal, and, Jeems, some whiskey; and we'll go unto
your mistress, Jeems.' And Jeems harnessed up the
cart, and we started. It was late at night, sir, when
we got there; so I said to Jeems, 'Jeems, it's no use
to unload the cart to-night. Put the horse in the
stable, Jeems, and unload the cart in the mornin'.'

"And Jeems said, 'Yes, massa.'

"I met my wife, sir; I embraced her, and went to
bed. Next mornin', *Jeems was gone!* Then I
came here; and the first thing I saw when I got
here was Jeems, a-peddlin' cabbages to your men, out
of that very cart!"

The general and his staff were sorry for the poor old man who had been so fearfully deceived in regard to the amount of affection his slaves had entertained for him ; but the amusing features of the case, as he presented it, predominated, and a general laugh followed.

The old Virginian did not laugh. On the contrary, he turned on his heel, and left the fort, without another word being said on either side.

On the 27th of May, Gen. Butler wrote to the War Department, that, in his opinion, Richmond could be reached and captured by way of the James River.

He said, " I have a force of six thousand men ; but I have no horses or wagons, and I shall need a large number of surf-boats for landing my men, &c." In this communication he presented a carefully prepared and elaborate plan of his proposed campaign, which he was confident, and is still confident, would have been successful had the means asked for been furnished, but they were not. He was even obliged to order nine of his own horses from his home at Lowell, as a matter of pressing necessity. No amount of asking, urging, or any thing else, not even the influence of official friends at the seat of government, could influence the commander-in-chief to furnish this brave and active soldier the means of striking an effective blow.

A gentleman occupying a high position in the War Office wrote Gen. Butler, " I told the President to-day that —— would never let you have troops and means to make a decisive blow; and I read the de-

spatch, to show that I understood my man. He intended to treat you as he did, and as he has always
treated those who he knew would be effective if he
gave them the means. He retains every thing in his
own power, and under his own immediate control, so
as to monopolize all the reputation to be made."

THE BATTLE OF GREAT BETHEL.

Gen. Butler became impatient under such treatment, and resolved to strike for his country. This
seemed necessary, for the reason that the rebels were
growing bold, and might conclude to attack his lines
ere long. Indeed, they were sending out squads, and
capturing Union men and negroes daily.

They had fortified two points near by, — Great
Bethel and Little Bethel; and Gen. Butler resolved
upon the capture of these posts, though his positive
orders limited him to a half-day's march from his
headquarters.

The plans were well laid; but he had no cavalry,
very little artillery, and not an officer or soldier who
had ever been in battle.

He gave the chief command to Gen. E. W. Pierce,
formerly his senior officer in the Massachusetts
militia. Parton says, "This was by way of atone-
ment to Gen. Pierce for having taken the place which
by seniority belonged to him, and was honorable to
his feelings as a man, but a blunder in a military
point of view. Gen. Pierce was a brave and good
man, but at that time wholly unfit for so responsible

a duty." It were needless to repeat the history of that day's blunders. Suffice it that the expedition proved a failure; and our troops, sent out in detach- ments at night, fired on each other on two different occasions, and finally retreated before the rebels, after the loss of some twenty men, including among the killed Major Winthrop and Lieut. Greble.

Many blunders of greater magnitude have been made since; but this was the first, and it attracted universal attention. Gen. Pierce was so mortified at his failure, that, at the end of the three-months' campaign, he enlisted for three years as a private soldier, with a determination to serve his country, which proved his patriotism and his courage, and with the sensible resolve to take some lessons in obeying orders before again attempting to command. He proved so excellent a soldier, that, by dint of merit, he rose to the command of a regiment, and was severely wounded while riding at the head of his command in one of the battles of the Penin- sula.

To Gen. Butler the defeat at Great Bethel was full of lessons. He felt badly about it, of course; but reflection led him to the conclusion that it was just what might have been expected under the circum- stances, hampered and embarrassed as he was by want of means to make aggressive war, and with none but undisciplined troops, who had not been under fire, hence subject to panic on the slightest occasion. One of the important lessons he learned was this, that raw troops are not to be relied upon in

an engagement, unless commanded by veteran officers in whom they have implicit confidence.

The author agrees with James Parton, in the
opinion that the greatest misfortune to the country
resulting from this affair was, that, through the exag-
gerations and misrepresentations of the public press
at a time when public attention was, centred almost
exclusively upon him, it served to cast a shadow
upon the fame of the greatest general then in the
service, concealing temporarily his real merits. Complete success here, following his brilliant career at
Annapolis and Baltimore, would undoubtedly have
forced him into such prominent popularity, that the
American people would have demanded for him a
leading position in the conduct of the war.

Gen. Butler was not the sort of man that permits
a single repulse to cool his ardor, or destroy his
confidence in plans he knows to be wisely formed.
He still had unshaken confidence in his previously
formed opinion, that the way to Richmond was by
the James River; and his preparations for sweeping
the rebels from the Virginia part of the Peninsula
went forward with unabated activity. But, just as he
felt himself prepared to make a formidable advance,
the battle of Bull Run occurred; and this disgraceful
disaster was followed immediately by a despatch from
Gen. Scott to Gen. Butler to send to Washington the
bulk and the flower of his army, including Col. Baker
and his command. Of course the expedition was
abandoned.

The news of the battle of Bull Run, and the withdrawal of a large part of the force from Fortress Monroe, left that post in an exposed position; but Gen. Butler was not frightened. He wrote: "We have heard the sad news ·from Manassas, but are neither dismayed nor disheartened. It will have the same good effect upon the army in general that Big Bethel has had upon my division, — to teach wherein we are weak, and the rebels strong, and how to apply the remedy to our deficiencies. Let not the administration be discouraged; let no mourning be felt, or compromises be made. God helping, we will go through to assured success. But let us have no more of the silk glove in carrying on this war. Let these men be considered what they have made themselves, — our enemies; and let their property of all kinds, whenever it can be useful to us, be taken on the land, as they take ours on the sea. There seems to me now but one of two ways, — either to make an advance from this place with sufficient force, or else, leaving a simple garrison here, to send six thousand men that might be spared on the other line, or still another to make a descent upon the southern coast. I am ready and desirous to move forward in either."

His letter won him the friendship of the radicals, his old-time political foes, but was not at all popular among the conservatives with whom he had affiliated all his life. Lewis Tappan wrote him a letter full of praise for his patriotic sentiments. In his reply he said, "I have endeavored to do my duty, following the best light I have; and the event must be in the hands of Him who ordereth all things well."

SUPPRESSING THE LIQUOR-TRAFFIC.

The author cannot afford, even in so brief a work as this must necessarily be, to omit an account of Gen. Butler's successful efforts in suppressing drunkenness in his command. He observed that the pickets would often go on duty perfectly sober, and come in very drunk. He could not guess where they got the liquor, as their canteens were free from the smell of it. It was finally observed that they carried their guns very perpendicularly, and this led to the discovery that the barrels were full of whiskey. The general, on instituting a vigorous search, found that the sutler was keeping a private saloon. It was short work for him, and he did it personally, to knock in the heads of some half-dozen barrels of all sorts of liquors, and turn the contents on the thirsty ground. He found the book containing the private account of the sutler with his officers, for whiskey, brandy, &c., and was astonished and mortified to find that nearly every officer in his command had accounts against him, some of which were very large. The drinking had been done almost solely at Newport News: hence it had in large part escaped the personal notice of the general. But, on getting possession of this book, he went to Newport News; and, calling his officers together, he exhibited the documentary proof of their guilt, and then proceeded to deliver a very eloquent and forcible temperance-lecture. He pointed out the evils of such conduct, and not only urged that a

stop be put to drinking in his department, but assured them that he meant to put a stop to it.   He
gave his solemn pledge, on the honor of an officer
and a man, that all that could intoxicate should be
banished from his own quarters; and he earnestly
hoped that they would join their commander in this
pledge.   They did so unanimously, with a single exception; and the resignation of this obstinate captain was instantly handed in and accepted.

GENERAL BUTLER CAPTURES FORT HATTERAS.

While Gen. Butler was chafing under his wrongs
at having his plans all spoiled by being deprived of a
large part of his force, he suddenly found himself
relieved of his command by Gen. Wool.   The order
from headquarters relieving him did not assign him
to duty anywhere else, nor even instruct him to report at Washington.   He therefore remained at Fort
Monroe, and accepted service under Gen. Wool, who,
recognizing his ability, gave him the command of the
volunteer forces, comprising five regiments and two
battalions.   He had been planning the reduction of
Fort Hatteras, and to this work Gen. Wool now assigned him.   His brilliant success in this expedition
is a matter of familiar history.   The work was done
promptly and done well; but he now found himself
out of employment, and West Point influence had by
this time grown so potent that it looked as though
all effective volunteer generals were to be either retired from the service, or put where they could not

do any thing to demonstrate their superiority over the kid-glove military aristocracy.

These gentry soon found that Gen. Butler was one of the irrepressibles. He obtained from the Secretary of War permission to recruit a force in Massachusetts with a view to carrying out his plan of driving the rebels from the Peninsula; but on reaching Boston he was informed by Gov. Andrew, that he had promised Gen. Sherman all new regiments that might be raised in that State for some time to come. Before learning this he had announced a war speech for Faneuil Hall; but, finding himself checkmated by the wily old sachem Tecumseh, he withdrew the appointment, and left for Washington, saying, "I go for a vigorous prosecution of the war, as evidence of which I am gone." This had a double meaning. He recognized the fact that he had two hosts of foes to contend with, — the armed rebels, and the regular army ring which had resolved to monopolize all the glory and other advantages incident to the war. He asked the Secretary of War for a recruiting commission covering the whole of New England. It was granted, with permission to raise six regiments, and to arm them as he pleased. Lest this might be revoked, he sought and obtained the President's indorsement of this order. On returning to Boston, Gov. Andrew objected to his entering the field in competition with Gen. Sherman, and a coolness arose; but, on the governor's own proposition, Gen. Butler agreed to wait a week, for Gen. Sherman's regiments to be filled, he in the mean time beginning operations in Maine. In the mean time, by order of Gen. Scott, the six New-England States were erected into a military department, and placed under the command of Major-Gen. B. F. Butler, with head-quarters at Boston. This proved offensive to Gov. Andrew, who held that Gen. Butler was interfering with his prerogative as governor and commander-in-chief of the militia of the State; and he threw all the obstacles possible in Gen. Butler's way, refusing to commission his officers, &c. The quarrel was an unfortunate one; but while we regard Gov. Andrew a good man, who had the best interest of the country at heart, he was not entirely free from those faults so common to all men, partisan preference and personal ambition. He was piqued at Gen. Butler for over-riding his authority with his order from the War Department; and he desired, if he did commission officers in Massachusetts regiments, such officers should be selected by himself, and not by Gen. But-ler. Gen. Butler, on the other hand, was faithfully doing his duty under orders from the War Depart-ment, as a recruiting officer, with the expectation of commanding the men he was recruiting: hence he wanted the various regiments commanded by good officers, men whom he knew and in whom he could have confidence. Hard words were said. The news-papers magnified and misrepresented the matter. The result was such delay of Gen. Butler's opera-tions that the carrying-out of his scheme to clear the Peninsula of rebels fell to Gen. Dix, who got the glory which would, and rightfully should, have rested upon the head of Gen. Butler.

He went to Washington to see what there was for
him to do. He was asked to report a plan for the
capture of Mobile. He did so: it was accepted, and
he ordered to enter upon the expedition. He returned to Boston, started Gen. Phelps for Ship Island;
back to Washington, to find his plan out of favor,
and himself called upon to prepare a plan for a Texas
campaign. He did so; and Gen. McClellan said
it was able, lucid, and complete. Home again for
more troops, for Texas this time. "The Constitution," which had borne Gen. Phelps to Ship Island,
had returned. He resolved to send her to Texas,
with two regiments. He had got them on board,
when a despatch from Washington was received. It
read, "*Don't sail! Disembark!*"

The cause of this sudden change of programme
was the demand of Great Britain for the surrender
of Mason and Slidell, who had been captured on a
British vessel, and were now prisoners in Fort Warren. It was probable that war with England might
demand his services, and the services of his troops
in Canada. He was ready for this. He opposed
strongly the idea of yielding to the demand for the
surrender of these arch traitors in obedience to an
insulting threat from an arrogant nation, which had
shown itself in sympathy with the rebels from the
first. He, with many others, thought that a war with
England, if it should come to that, would unify and
strengthen us as a nation. He said, "I can raise
fifty thousand additional men in New England alone,
who will follow me into Canada before England can

land a single soldier there, and take possession of and hold that province against the combined fleet of Great Britain." A different policy prevailed, however. Mason and Slidell were surrendered, and this new war-cloud passed away; and Gen. Butler sailed with his command to Fortress Monroe, where they were destined to remain inactive for a long time, due partly to an important change in the War Office, Mr. Cameron going out, and Mr. Stanton coming in.

Secretary Stanton entered upon his new duties with a determination to prosecute the war with vigor: hence he naturally sought an important field of operations for so brave and energetic a general as Butler. On the 10th of January, 1862, Secretary Stanton electrified Gen. Butler by asking him the question, "Why can't New Orleans be taken?"

"*It can*," responded the general. "I've thought of it before."

"Prepare a plan, said the secretary; and Gen. Butler set to work in high hopes that now an expedition worthy of his metal was about to be offered him.

Gen. McClellan advised against it, saying, "It will take fifty thousand men, and that force cannot be spared."

Gen. Butler went to the White House; and, by dint of such eloquence and logic as he alone knows how to use, he won the President. His joy almost overcame him. But Gen. McClellan refused to give him a single soldier from the idle army of two hundred thousand then at Washington. But his troops at Fort Monroe were available, and he had eighty-five hundred still in New England ; and finally, after some delays, the Department of the Gulf was created, and Major-Gen. Benjamin F. Butler assigned to the command.

On the 24th of February he left Washington for his new field of labor, — a field yet to be conquered. His force consisted of 15,255 men, mostly raw troops from New England, but including the 21st Indiana, 4th Wisconsin, and 6th Michigan, — all veterans.

His destination and plans were a profound secret between the heads of the departments at Washington, himself, Major Strong, and Lieut. Weitzel of his staff.

The general's wife had shared his camp-life from the first, and she bravely volunteered to accompany him on this perilous expedition.

CHAPTER VII.

THE CAPTURE OF NEW ORLEANS.

AFTER a stormy voyage of a month, and many adventures, Gen. Butler landed on Ship Island, a strip of land seven miles in length, and less than one in width, situated sixty-five miles below New Orleans. It was now the last of March, and in this Southern clime the weather was very sultry; insects were numerous, and but few comforts to be had to offset the numerous discomforts. But Gen. Butler and his men were not pleasure-seekers: they were soldiers whose determined purpose it was to capture and hold New Orleans. Capt. Farragut was there with his fleet, ready to co-operate in this grand scheme; and preparations were entered upon with vigor. Capt. Farragut said he could be ready to move on Forts Jackson and St. Philip in a week; and Gen. Butler undertook to be ready also to move in that time, though an immense amount of work was to be done. He worked night and day, heartily seconded by his officers and soldiers.

The obstacles between these land and naval forces and the city of New Orleans were many and formidable, — the two forts mounting a hundred and twenty heavy guns, fully manned, and amply supplied with ammunition; an immense cable stretched across the channel, immediately below Fort Jackson, which must be cut before a vessel could pass that point; and above this, the rebel fleet of vessels, iron-clads, and rams.

The rebel commanders felt confident that they could defend the approaches to the city against the combined naval force of the world : hence they were disposed to laugh at the preparations of Capt. Farragut and Gen. Butler.

On the 17th of April the fleet stood in battle array, four miles below Fort Jackson. The guns of the fort opened upon it, but Capt. Farragut did not reply for some hours. He and his men had enough to do to destroy the numerous fire-rafts sent down upon them by the rebels; but in the afternoon a few of the mortar-boats were allowed to open on the fort. The next morning at daybreak the battle began in earnest; the mortar-boats having moved up, and taken positions from one and a half to two and a half miles from Fort St. Philip. A newspaper-correspondent who witnessed the battle from a lofty position on the flagship describes it as highly interesting and grand. Immense balls were whizzing through the air, and falling like meteoric globes about the boats, plashing the water in all directions. The masts of the vessels were crowded with men, eager to see what effect our shots were having upon the fort; and, when a two-hundred-pound shell would drop in among the rebel gunners, a shout would go up from these spectators. The battle raged unabated for two days, when Gen. Butler, who had been an anxious looker-on from below, visited Capt. Farragut on the flagship "Hartford;" and after a conference it was decided that the cable must be cut, and the forts passed in the night under cover of darkness, for it was now evident that they could not be reduced by bombardment. On the next night Capt. Bell with two gunboats, the "Pinola" and "Itasca," ran up to the cable, and cut it.

During this operation, which lasted an hour and a half, Capt. Porter kept up a furious bombardment of the forts, with a view of attracting attention from Capt. Bell's little fleet; but this was not successful. Capt. Bell was discovered, and a heavy fire opened on him from the rebel batteries. He paid no attention to it, however; but he and his brave men worked with determined energy, until the mighty iron cable parted, leaving the channel of the river again navigable. He then dropped down, and made report to his commander.

Preparations now went forward, looking to the desperate venture of running the gauntlet between these two forts. The battle, however, still continued with unabated vigor on both sides. It lasted a hundred and forty-nine hours.

At two o'clock on the night of the 23d of April the signal was given, and the fleet began to move. Every thing had been prepared for the most rapid fire possible during the hour and a quarter necessary to pass the forts; and during that time from five to eight of those monster two-hundred-pound shells were in the air constantly, and the roar, the crash, the smoke, were terrific. Just as the first ship, "The Cayuga," passed the cable, the design was obvious to the rebels; and both forts opened on the fleet with every gun. The bombs and shot fell around the ships like hail; but the ships and gunboats held on their way, each giving the fort a broadside as it passed. The forts passed, Capt. Farragut found himself hotly engaged by the rebel fleet of ships, gunboats, and iron-clad monsters, including the "Morgan" and "Manassas." Numerous fire-rafts were also hurled upon him; but he was fully prepared for these, hence but little damage was done by them. In the midst of the battle, the flagship took fire.

"This [says a correspondent of "The Herald"] was the crowning moment of this unparalleled fight. It was beyond description. Twenty mortars, a hundred and forty-two guns in the fleet, a hundred and twenty on the forts, the crash of splinters, the explosion of boilers and magazines, the cries, the shrieks of scalded and drowning men, the belching flashes of the guns, the blazing rafts, the burning steamboats, the river full of fire, — all combined to produce a spectacle of unparalleled grandeur and terror. But, if it was terrible, it was of short duration; for the forts were passed, and the rebel fleet destroyed and captured, in an hour and a half. 'The Cayuga' had been struck forty-two times, damaging her rigging considerably; but Capt. Bailey ran ashore five miles above the forts, and captured a quarantine station, and, as the other ships came to anchor, repeated shouts of victory rent the morning air. It is a remarkable fact, that, except 'The Itasca' and 'Varuna,' not a .

vessel in the fleet had been seriously injured. Gen. Butler witnessed this splendid naval engagement from the deck of 'The Saxon;' and, when it ended, he dropped down to his transports, which were put in motion, with the purpose of landing the troops back of and above Fort St. Philip; for it will be borne in mind that the forts had not been captured. On the morning of the 26th, Gen. Butler having landed, the forts were invested on all sides. The same evening news reached the general that Capt. Farragut had anchored his fleet in the harbor of New Orleans; and, leaving Gen. Williams in command of his troops, he, in company with Capt. Boggs, went up to the city. That night a large body of rebel troops came in, and surrendered to Butler's forces; and the next morning the officers of the forts made a formal surrender to Capt. Porter. The victory was now complete, and Gen. Butler was master of New Orleans. Justice requires that the glory of this grand achievement should be shared mutually by Gen. Butler and Capt. Farragut."

Parton says, —

"If the splendid daring of Capt. Farragut and his fleet deprived Gen. Butler of his lieutenant-generalship, it is but just to him to declare that the prompt and unexpected landing of the troops in the rear of Fort St. Philip compelled the surrender of the forts. Fighting wins laurels, but a manoeuvre that accomplishes results without fighting also merits recognition."

Yes; and when the historian shall write for *truly* civilized readers, the fame of the commander who achieves triumphs without bloodshed will rank far above that of the chieftain who hurls his army upon the foe regardless of danger to himself or others.

CHAPTER VIII.

GEN. BUTLER'S CAREER IN NEW ORLEANS.

THE chief characteristics of Gen. Butler are honesty of purpose, calm deliberation, wise and comprehensive judgment, and firm and prompt executive force. He does nothing hastily, nothing that he thinks is wrong; but, when his mind is made up, he acts with vigor: hence, when placed in an important position, those who agree with him admire him, but those who oppose his views hate him. There can be no middle ground of indifference from which to contemplate a character so great and so positive as he. In the light of this analysis, it is easy to understand why his most admirable, almost faultless, administration at New Orleans should have provoked such bitter denunciations and extravagant misrepresentations from the rebels and their sympathizers in this country and Europe, while it won him the gratitude of the President and all intelligent patriots throughout the whole country. The population of New Orleans was composed almost wholly of aristocrats and roughs. With rare exceptions the people were extremely excitable and intensely disloyal.

When it was known in the city that the forts had surrendered, the rebel navy had been destroyed, and Gen. Butler was on his way to take possession of the city, ex-senator Soulé advised the burning of all the cotton and other merchandise on the levee and the steamers in the harbor, and with his own hand he began the work of destruction by applying a lighted torch to a pile of cotton-bales belonging to himself; and it is estimated that not less than two hundred and fifty thousand bales of cotton, besides an immense amount of other property, were destroyed. And, when Capt. Farragut came in view of the city, the whole seven miles of wharf was a sea of fire; and but for the active efforts of what was styled the "European Brigade," composed of non-residents, the city would have suffered general pillage and destruction before our forces landed.

Capt. Farragut sent a message to Mayor Monroe, demanding the formal surrender of the city, and the running-up of the stars and stripes instead of the rebel flag on the public buildings. The reply was a peremptory refusal from Gen. Lovell, the rebel commander, who said, "he had evacuated the city, but refused to surrender it; and if Capt. Farragut chose to shell the town, destroying women and children, he was at liberty to do so."

This was simply contemptible and insulting; but he was assured that the object was to protect the city and its people, not destroy.

Gen. Lovell immediately left the city, after delivering himself of this chivalrous speech; and the mayor refused to hoist the American flag, adding, "There lives not in this city a wretched renegade who would so far demean himself as to lower the emblem of our aspirations." Capt. Farragut sent a force on shore with instructions to raise the emblem of the United States on the Custom House and other public buildings, which was done; and the mob were informed, that, if the flags were interfered with, the buildings would be instantly fired upon from the fleet.

On Sunday, while the men on board were at worship, the notorious gambler Mumford, assisted by three others, tore down the flag from its staff on the Mint, and, after dragging it through the street till it was covered with filth, tore it in pieces.

The men on the lookout of "The Pensacola" saw the act, and pulled the cords of the guns all along the broadside, but the wafers had been removed, and the guns were not discharged, which fortunate circumstance saved many lives.

"The Picayune" next morning glorified the act, saying, —

"The names of the men who distinguished themselves by gallantly tearing down the flag that has been surreptitiously hoisted are W. B. Mumford, Lieut. N. Holmes, Sergeant Burns, and James Reed. These men deserve great credit for their patriotic act," &c.

Gen. Butler arrived a few hours after the flag had been torn down; and if he had been the rash and cruel man he was afterwards described by the rebels, North and South, he would have ordered the city shelled for such an outrage.

He saw clearly that such a lawless spirit must be suppressed : hence he advised the captain to threaten bombardment if any more insults should be offered the American flag ; and, as a preliminary, he ordered the women and children to leave town.

On the 1st of May, Gen. Butler, having returned to his transports to bring his command to the city, landed at New Orleans with his entire force.

Before permitting the troops to go on shore, the following was read : —

HEADQUARTERS DEPARTMENT OF THE GULF,
NEW ORLEANS, May 1, 1862.

GENERAL ORDER NO. 15.

I. In anticipation of the immediate disembarkation of the troops of this command amid the temptations and inducements of a large city, all plundering of public or private property, by any person or persons, is hereby forbidden under the severest penalties.

II. No officer or soldier will absent himself from his station, without arms or alone, under any pretext whatever.

III. The commanders of regiments and companies will be held responsible for the strict execution of these orders.

" By command of

MAJOR-GEN. BUTLER.

GEORGE C. STRONG, *A. A. G.*

The general also gave strict orders that no officer or soldier should resent any insult, or reply to any taunt.

Gen. Butler landed with the first detachment, and marched to the Custom House to the music of a band which played " The Star-spangled Banner." The crowd which filled the streets, and followed the line of march, showered profane and vulgar epithets upon him, and cheered for Beauregard; but no notice was taken of them. The following proclamation, which was set up and printed by Union soldiers in the "True Delta" office, — the proprietors of the office refusing to do the job, — furnishes a clear insight into Gen. Butler's policy : —

PROCLAMATION OF GEN. BUTLER.

HEADQUARTERS DEPARTMENT OF THE GULF,
NEW ORLEANS, May 1, 1862.

The city of New Orleans and its environs, with all its interior and exterior defences, having surrendered to the com-bined naval and land forces of the United States, and being now in the occupation of the forces of the United States, who have come to restore order, maintain public tranquillity, and en-force peace and quiet under the laws and constitution of the United States, the major-general commanding hereby proclaims the object and purposes of the Government of the United States in thus taking possession of New Orleans and the State of Louisiana, and the rules and regulations by which the laws of the United States will be for the present, and during the state of war, enforced and maintained for the plain guidance of all good citizens of the United States, as well as all others who may have heretofore been in rebellion against their authority.

Thrice before has the city of New Orleans been rescued from the hands of a foreign government, and still more calamitous domestic insurrection, by the money and arms of the United States. It has of late been under the military control of the rebel forces; and at each time, in the judgment of the com-manders of the military forces holding it, it has been found necessary to preserve order and maintain quiet by an adminis-tration of martial law. Even during the interim from its evac-uation by the rebel soldiers, and its actual possession by the soldiers of the United States, the civil authorities have found

It necessary to call for the intervention of an armed body, known as the European Legion, to preserve the public tranquillity. The commanding general, therefore, will cause the city to be guarded until the restoration of the United States authority and his further orders by martial law.

All persons in arms against the United States are required to surrender themselves, with their arms, equipments, and munitions of war. The body known as the European Legion, not being understood to be in arms against the United States, but organized to protect the lives and property of the citizens, are invited to still co-operate with the forces of the United States to that end, and, so acting, will not be included in the terms of ' this order, but will report to these headquarters.

All ensigns, flags, devices, tending to uphold any authority whatever, save the flags of the United States and those of foreign consulates, must not be exhibited, but suppressed. The American ensign, the emblem of the United States, must be treated with the utmost deference and respect by all persons, under pain of severe punishment.

All persons well disposed towards the Government of the United States, who shall renew the oath of allegiance, will receive a safeguard of protection to their persons and property from the army of the United States, and the violation of such safeguard will be punishable with death. All persons still holding allegiance to the Confederate States will be deemed rebels against the Government of the United States, and regarded and treated as enemies thereof.

All foreigners not naturalized, and claiming allegiance to their respective governments, and not having made oath of allegiance to the Government of the Confederate States, will be protected in their persons and property, as heretofore, under the laws of the United States. All persons who may have heretofore given adherence to the supposed government of the Confederate States, or been in their service, who shall lay down or deliver up their arms, return to peaceful occupations, and preserve quiet and order, holding no further correspondence, nor giving aid and comfort to enemies of the United States, will not be disturbed in their persons or property, except so far under the orders of the commanding general as the exigencies of the public service mãy render necessary.

Keepers of all public property, whether State, National, or Confederate, such as collections of art, libraries, and museums, as well as all public buildings, all munitions of war, and armed vessels, will at once make full returns thereof to these headquarters. All manufacturers of arms and munitions of war will report to these headquarters their kind and places of business. All the rights of property, of whatever kind, will be held inviolate, subject only to the laws of the United States. All the inhabitants are enjoined to pursue their usual avocations. All shops and places of amusement are to be kept open in the accustomed manner, and services are to be held in the churches and religious houses, as in times of profound peace.

Keepers of all public houses and drinking-saloons are to report their names and numbers to the office of the provost-marshal; and they will then receive a license, and be held responsible for all disorders and disturbances arising in their respective places.

Sufficient force will be kept in the city to preserve order and maintain the laws. The killing of American soldiers by any disorderly person or mob is simply assassination and murder, and not war, and will be so regarded and punished. The owner of any house in which such murder shall be committed will be held responsible therefor, and the house be liable to be destroyed by the military authority. All disorders, disturbances of the peace, and crimes of an aggravated nature, interfering with the forces or laws of the United States, will be referred to a military court for trial and punishment. Other misdemeanors will be subject to the municipal authority, if it desires to act.

Civil causes between party and party will be referred to the ordinary tribunals.

The levy and collection of taxes, save those imposed by the laws of the United States, are suppressed, except those for keeping in repair and lighting the streets, and for sanitary purposes. These are to be collected in the usual manner.

The circulation of Confederate bonds, evidences of debt (except notes in the similitude of bank-notes), issued by the Confederate States, or scrip, or any trade in the same, is forbidden. It has been represented to the commanding general, by the civil authorities, that these Confederate notes, in the form of bank-notes, in a great measure are the only substitutes for money which the people have been allowed to have, and that great distress would ensue among the poorer classes if the circulation of such notes should be suppressed. Such circulation, therefore, will be permitted so long as any one will be inconsiderate enough to receive them, until further orders.

No publication of newspapers, pamphlets, or handbills, giving accounts of the movements of the soldiers of the United States within this department, reflecting in any way upon the United States, intended in any way to influence the public mind against the United States, will be permitted; and all articles on war news, editorial comments, or correspondence, making comments upon the movements of the armies of the United States, must be submitted to the examination of an officer, who will be detailed for that purpose from these headquarters. The transmission of all communications by telegraph will be under the charge of an officer detailed from these headquarters.

The armies of the United States came here not to destroy, but to restore order out of chaos, to uphold the government and laws in the place of the "passage" of men. To this end, therefore, the efforts of all well disposed are invited, to have every species of disorder quelled.

If any soldier of the United States should so far forget his duty or his flag as to commmit outrage upon any person or property, the commanding general requests his name to be instantly reported to the provost-guard, so that he may be punished, and his wrongful act redressed. The municipal authority, so far as the police of the city and environs are concerned, is to extend as before indicated until suspended.

All assemblages of persons in the streets, either by day or night, tend to disorder, and are forbidden.

The various companies composing the Fire Department of

New Orleans will be permitted to retain their organizations, and are to report to the provost-marshal, so that they may be known, and not interfered with in their duties.

And finally, it may be sufficient to add, without further enumeration, that all the requirements of martial law will be imposed so long as, in judgment of the United States authorities, it may be necessary; and, while it is desired by these authorities to exercise this government mildly, and after the usages of the past, it must not be supposed that it will not be rigorously and firmly administered as the occasion calls for it.

By command of

MAJOR-GEN. BUTLER.

GEORGE B. STRONG, *A.A.G., Chief of Staff.*

The next day the general established his headquarters in the St. Charles Hotel, and notified Mayor Monroe that he should be glad to have a conference with him. At two o'clock, the mayor, Pierre Soulé, and quite a party of leading men, waited upon the general in the ladies' parlor, which he had taken for his office.

The interview had scarce begun when an aide to Gen. Williams, who was in command of the guard which had been placed about the hotel, came in to say that the general feared he would not be able to control the mob. Gen. Butler replied, —

"Give my compliments to Gen. Williams, and tell him, if he cannot control the mob, to open upon them with artillery."

"Don't do that," exclaimed Mayor Monroe and several other Southern men.

"Why not, gentlemen? The mob must be controlled. We can't have disturbance in the street."

"Shall I go out, and speak to the people?" asked the mayor.

"As you please: I only insist on having order."

The mayor and Mr. Soulé made short speeches, but it had very little effect.

The mayor then said to Gen. Butler, "You were formerly an advocate of the rights of the South. We looked upon you as our special friend and champion."

"Stop, sir," said the general: "I was always a friend of Southern rights, but a foe to Southern wrongs."

At this point Lieut. Kinsman of the general's staff came in, accompanied by Judge Summers, a loyal citizen, who had fled to the fleet for protection from the mob, and now had ventured ashore under the lieutenant's protection, and whose life had been threatened, and was only saved by the officer's valor and courage, while getting from the landing to the hotel.

The judge was so badly frightened that he did not feel safe even in the St. Charles; and the general ordered the officer to summon a file of soldiers, and escort him to the Custom House.

On reaching the side door, the judge thought the fifty soldiers inadequate to the task of protecting him from the immense and highly excited mob; and he begged the lieutenant not to attempt to take him to the Custom House. "But my orders are positive," he replied: "I must obey." The soldiers were formed in two lines, four feet apart, with two in front and two behind, with the lieutenant and the judge in the centre. Thus they marched, keeping the mob

from the object of their vengeance by fixed bayonets. Two arrests were made of especially violent
fellows ; and these were quieted only by orders from
the officer to the soldiers, to run their bayonets into
them if they did not keep quiet. This affair had a
wholesome effect upon the New Orleans rebels.

The same evening Gen. Butler drove from the St.
Charles to the river, a distance of near a mile, without escort save a single orderly ; a fact which not
only illustrated the cool courage of the man, but the
fact that true courage is the best protection against
a cowardly mob. On the following day a second
conference was held between Gen. Butler and the
leading men of the city, the mayor and his board of
councilmen being present. The general explained
his views and plans very fully in regard to the situation, and his ideas of the government of the city;
and then politely invited a correspondingly frank
expression from them. He assured them that it was
his earnest wish that the municipal authorities should
exercise their lawful functions, leaving him simply
the duties of a military commander, whose business
it was to represent the National Government, and
sustain its authority against its foes.

Mr. Soulé replied, that the tranquillity of the city
could not be maintained while the troops remained
in it, and urged their immediate withdrawal. "The
people are not conquered, and cannot be expected to
act as a conquered people. Your soldiers cannot
have peace or safety in our midst."

Gen. Butler kept his temper as he replied, "I am

surprised to hear a threat from Mr. Soulé on an occasion of this sort. I have been accustomed to hear threats from Southern gentlemen in political conventions ; but I assure you gentlemen present, that the time for such tactics has passed, never to return. New Orleans *is* a conquered city : else how did we get here, and why are we here ? Did you open your arms, and bid us welcome ? Would you not expel us if you could ? No, gentlemen : New Orleans has been conquered by the forces of the United States, and by the laws of all nations is subject to the will of the conquerors. Nevertheless, when I propose to leave the municipal government to the free exercise of all its powers, I am answered by a threat. Gladly will I take every soldier out of the city the very hour it is demonstrated to me that the city government can and *will* protect me, and other loyal men, from insult and danger. Your inability or unwillingness to do this has been clearly shown by the treatment of my men this afternoon, and by the fact that Gen. Lovell was obliged to proclaim martial law while his army occupied your city, to protect law-abiding citizens from the rowdies.

"I therefore proclaim martial law, not against respectable citizens, but against the same class that Gen. Wilkinson, Gen. Jackson, and Gen. Lovell declared it. I understand the situation better, perhaps, than you think. I am aware of the existence of an organization here established for the express purpose of assassinating my men in detail ; but I warn you that if a shot is fired from any house, it will

never again shelter a mortal head, and if I can dis-
cover the perpetrator of the deed, the place that
knows him now shall know him no more forever. I
have the power to suppress the unruly element in
your midst; and I mean to use it so effectually that
in a short period I shall be able to traverse your
streets alone free from insult or peril, or else this
metropolis of the South shall be a desert from the
Plains of Chalmette to the outskirts of Carrollton."

The proclamation appeared the next day, Col. J.
H. French being named as provost-marshal, and
Major J. W. Bell as provost-judge.

During that day the foreign consuls waited upon
the general, and had a pleasant interview. A delegation of the city council also called to say that the
proposal from him, that the city government should
go on as usual, was accepted; and requesting the
withdrawal of the troops from the City Hall, that the
authorities might not seem to be acting under military dictation. This request was at once granted.
The general also sent Gen. Williams and Capt.
Farragut up to Baton Rouge, with instructions to
occupy and hold it. Camps were established out of
the city for the bulk of the army; so that in a short
time but two hundred and fifty men remained in it,
simply enough for a competent provost-guard.

In a few days all was comparatively quiet; and the
press, though still rebel, almost complimented Gen.
Butler in commenting upon the change. "The Bee"
of May the 8th said, "The Federal soldiers do not
seem to interfere with private property, and have

done nothing, that we are aware, to provoke difficulty. The usual nightly arrests for vagrancy and assaults, wounding and killing, have unquestionably been diminished. The city is as tranquil and peaceable as in the most quiet times." Thus it is evident that Gen. Butler's administration started well. We shall see, as we progress with this history, that it was characterized throughout by dignity, prudence, and wisdom, as well as firmness and patriotism.

CHAPTER IX.

GEN. BUTLER GIVES EMPLOYMENT TO THE POOR, THUS
PREVENTING BOTH FAMINE AND PESTILENCE.

WHEN Gen. Butler took command of New
Orleans, there was not sufficient provisions to
feed the people one month; and the necessaries of
life cost such fabulous prices that only the rich could
purchase them. The poor were therefore on the
borders of famine. Flour was selling for sixty dollars per barrel, and other articles corresponded in
price. This had resulted from two causes chiefly:
the war had destroyed the productiveness of the
country and the trade of the city, and the rebel van-
dalism had destroyed the accumulated stock of goods
to prevent the Union army from getting possession
of them.

There were at least fifty thousand poor people,
chiefly women and children, whose physical salvation
depended upon the wisdom and philanthropy of one
man, and that man hated and reviled as no man ever
had been in that city. Gen. Butler acted up to the
standard of the true Christian, by a practical adoption of the sentiment expressed by the Saviour as he

hung upon the cross. He forgave them on the ground of their ignorance, and resolved to save them from death by famine.

Mr. Parton says, "This object had precedence of all others during the first few days, after securing comparative quiet; but of course he could not give his whole attention to it. He strove to revive the business of the city, which was dead. Confidence in the honest intentions of the Union authorities did not exist: he endeavored to call it into being. The currency was deranged: he must rectify it. The secessionists were audaciously vigilant: he had to circumvent and repress them."

The yellow-fever season was at hand: he was resolved to ward off the pestilence. The city government was obstructive and hostile: it was his business to frustrate their endeavors. The negro problem loomed up vast and portentous: he must act upon it without delay. The banks were in disorder: their affairs demanded his attention. The consulates were so many centres of hostile operations: he had to penetrate their mysteries. His army was not large, his field of operation immense: he could not neglect the chief business of his mission to this Southern field of operations. He gave from his own purse one thousand dollars toward the immediate relief of the starving poor; and, on the suggestion of the city authorities, he gave permits to railroad and steamboat companies and traders to bring provisions into the city, the continuance of said permits being dependent upon their not giving intelligence, aid, or comfort

to the rebel forces.   For the faithful compliance with
this provision he had the pledge of the city authorities, and for its execution he held them responsible.
This obligation was violated in the most shameful
manner in numerous instances.   Provisions were
shipped to Gen. Lovell's troops, and spies passed to
and fro in the disguise of steamboat employees,
traders, &c.: still the good overbalanced the evil
of this plan.

The general had invited the attention of the mayor
to the filthy state of the city, and he and his council
agreed to have the streets cleaned ; but no such action
was taken, and he summoned the mayor to know why
this compact was not kept.   He said, "There are
plenty of idle men who could be profitably employed
in that work."

The mayor said that a force of three hundred men
had been set to work.   But no such force could
be seen by the general or his soldiers.   He therefore resolved to take the matter into his own hands
at once; and on the 9th of May he issued an order
to the effect that the city should employ the poor
laborers in the work of cleaning the streets, with a
view both to providing for the wants of the destitute,
and warding off pestilence.

This was sent to the City Council, who accepted
it as a good measure ; and a superintendent on behalf
of the city was appointed, Col. T. B. Thorpe being
named to act for the military authorities.   The party
named by the City Council refused to take the oath
of allegiance to the United States : hence Col. Thorpe

had sole charge of this work, which he pushed with energy and despatch.

Mr. Parton tells us that "Col. Thorpe's labors were of permanent benefit to the city in many ways. The Mississippi River is constantly adding new land to the city limits ; but this land requires considerable labor expended upon it before it is completely rescued from the domain of the river. It is estimated that Col. Thorpe's skilfully directed efforts added to the city an amount of available land worth one million of dollars."

Thus Gen. Butler not only gave relief to the poor in a legitimate way, but greatly benefited and permanently enriched the city by his plans of relief. His system resulted in more benefit to the city than expense, while it cost the United States not a cent. Secretary Chase wrote him, "You are the cheapest general we have employed."

GENERAL BUTLER'S ORIGINAL PLAN FOR RAISING MONEY.

Gen. Butler's plan is fully explained by the following order : —

AUG. 4, 1862.

It appears that the need of relief to the destitute poor of the city requires more extended measures and greater outlay than have yet been made.

It becomes a question in justice, Upon whom should this burden fall?

Clearly, upon those who have brought this great calamity upon their fellow-citizens.

It should not be borne by taxation of the whole municipality, because the middling and working men have never been heard at the ballot-box, unawed by threats and unmenaced by 'Thugs' and paid assassins of conspirators against peace and good order. Besides, more than the vote that was claimed for secession have taken the oath of allegiance to the United States.

The United-States Government does its share when it protects, defends, and preserves the people in the enjoyment of law, order, and calm quiet.

Those who have brought upon the city this stagnation of business, this desolation of the hearthstone, this starvation of the poor and helpless, should, as far as they may be able, relieve these distresses.

There are two classes whom it would seem peculiarly fit should at first contribute. First, those individuals and corporations who have aided the Rebellion with their means; and, second, those who have endeavored to destroy the commercial prosperity of the city, upon which the welfare of its inhabitants depend.

It is brought to the knowledge of the commanding general, that a subscription of twelve hundred and fifty thousand dollars was made by the corporate bodies, business firms, and persons whose names are set forth in Schedule "A" annexed to this order, and that sum placed in the hands of an illegal body known as the "Committee of Public Safety," for the treasonable purpose of defending the city against the Government of the United States, under whose humane rule the city of New Orleans had enjoyed such unexampled prosperity, that her warehouses were filled with fruits of all nations who come to share her freedom, to take part in the benefits of her commercial prosperity, and thus she was made the representative mart of the world.

The stupidity and wastefulness with which this immense sum was spent was only equalled by the folly which led to its being raised at all. The subscribers to this fund, by this very act, betray their treasonable designs, and their ability to pay at least a much smaller tax for the relief of their destitute and starving neighbors.

Schedule "B" is a list of cotton-brokers, who, claiming to

control that great interest in New Orleans, to which she is so much indebted for her wealth, published in the newspapers in October, 1861, a manifesto deliberately advising the planters not to bring their produce to the city; a measure which brought ruin at the same time upon the producer and the city.

This act sufficiently testifies the malignity of these traitors, as well to the Government as to their neighbors; and it is to be regretted that their ability to relieve their fellow-citizens is not equal to their facilities for injuring them.

In taxing both these classes to relieve the suffering poor of New Orleans, yea, even though the needy be the starving wives and children of those in arms at Richmond and elsewhere against the United States, it will be impossible to make a mistake save in having the assessment too easy and the burden too light.

It is therefore ordered : —

1st, That the sums in schedules annexed marked " A " and " B," set against the names of the several persons, business firms, and corporations herein described, be and hereby are assessed upon each respectively.

2d, That said sums be paid to Lieut. David C. G. Field, financial clerk, at his office in the Custom House, on or before Monday the 11th inst., or that the property of the delinquent be forthwith seized, and sold at public auction to pay the amount, with all necessary charges and expenses, or the party imprisoned till paid.

3d, The money raised by this assessment to be a fund for the purpose of providing employment and food for the deserving poor people of New Orleans.

[The first schedule embraced ninety-five names, as in the following.]

SCHEDULE A.

List of Contributors to the Million and a Quarter Loan, placed in the Hands of the so-called Committee of Public Safety, for the defence of New Orleans against the United States, and of which $38,000 about had been disbursed.

	Sums subscribed to aid treason against the United States.	Sums assessed to relieve the poor by the United States.
Abat, Generes, & Co.	$210,000	$52,500
Jonathan Montgomery	40,000	10,000
Thomas Sloo, President Sun Insurance Co. . .	50,000	12,500
C. C. Gaines	2,000	500
C. C. Gaines & Co.	3,000	750

[Total amount yielded under this item of assessment was $312,716.25.]

SCHEDULE B.

List of Cotton-Brokers of New Orleans who published in " The Crescent," in October last, a Card advising Planters not to send Produce to New Orleans, in order to induce Foreign Intervention in behalf of the Rebellion.

	Sums assessed to relieve the starving poor by the United States.
Hewitt, Norton, & Co.	$500
West & Villerie	250
S. E. Belknap	100
Brander, Chambliss, & Co.	500
Lewis & Oglesby	100

[The sum realized by this assessment was $29,200.

The effect of this order, No. 55, put at the disposal of Gen. Butler, for the purposes named, the sum of $341,916.25.]

These orders were hailed with joy by the poor, and muttered curses from the rich. The first saw in them promise of work and wages, hence relief from famine ; the latter, the stern necessity of yielding up some of their hoarded wealth, wrung from slave-labor, for the public good. "The True Delta" said to these men, "The poor must be employed and fed; you cannot be permitted to lie on cushioned divans, dining on turtle, and sipping choice wines, while hungry men and starving women and children walk the ever-busy streets in idleness."

The consuls representing the various European governments were all in active sympathy with secession, and these threw every possible obstruction in Gen. Butler's way. They lent willing ears to rebel complaints, and forwarded protests to the Secretary of State at Washington. But the general vindicated himself most successfully by a letter to the Secretary of War, closing as follows : —

"When I took possession of New Orleans I found the city nearly on the verge of starvation; the poor being utterly without means of procuring what food there was to be had. I endeavored to aid the city government in the work of feeding the poor; but I soon found that the very distribution of food was a means faithlessly used to encourage the Rebellion. I was obliged, therefore, to take the whole matter into my own hands. It had become a subject of alarming importance and gravity. It became necessary to provide, from some source, the funds to procure the food. They could not be raised by city taxation in the ordinary form. These taxes were in arrears to more than one million of dollars. Besides, it would be unjust to tax the loyal citizens and honestly neutral foreigners to provide for a state of things brought about by the rebels and disloyal foreigners, who had conspired together to overthrow the authority of the United States, and establish the very result which was to be met.

"Further, in order to have a contribution effective, it must be upon those who have wealth to meet it. There seems to be no such fit subjects for such taxation as the cotton-brokers who had brought the distress upon the city by paralyzing commerce, and the subscribers to the rebel loan.

"With these convictions I issued General Order No. 55, which will explain itself, and have raised nearly the amount of the tax therein set forth. But for what purpose? Not a dollar has gone in any way to the use of the United States. I am now employing one thousand poor laborers, as matter of charity, upon the streets and wharves of the city, from this fund. I am distributing food to preserve from starvation nine thousand seven hundred and seven families, containing thirty-two thousand four hundred souls, daily; and this at an expense of seventy thousand dollars per month. I am sustaining, at an expense of two thousand dollars per month, five asylums for widows and orphans. I am aiding the charity hospital to the extent of five thousand dollars per month.

"Before their Excellencies, the French and Prussian ministers, complain of my exactions upon foreigners at New Orleans, I desire that they should look at the documents, and consider for a moment the facts and figures set forth in this report. They will find that out of ten thousand four hundred and ninety families who have been fed from the fund, with the raising of which they find fault, *less than one-tenth* are Americans; nine thousand four hundred and eighty are foreigners. Of the thirty-two thousand souls, but three thousand are natives. Besides the charity at the asylums and hospitals, distributed in about the same proportion to foreign and native born; so that, of an expenditure of near eighty thousand dollars per month to employ and feed the starving poor of New Orleans, seventy-two thousand dollars goes to foreigners, whose compatriots loudly complain, and offensively thrust forward their neutrality, whenever they are called upon to aid their suffering countrymen.

"I should need no extraordinary taxation to feed the poor of New Orleans, if the bellies of the foreigners were as actively with the rebels as are the heads of those who claim exemption thus far from this taxation, made and used for the purposes above set forth, upon the ground of their neutrality; among whom I find Rochereau & Co., the senior partner of which firm took an oath of allegiance to the Constitution of the Confederate States. I find also the house of Riechard & Co., the senior partner of which, Gen. Riechard, is in the rebel army. I find the junior partner, Mr. Kruttschmidt, the brother-in-law of Benjamin, the rebel secretary of war, using all the funds in his hands to purchase arms, and collecting securities of his correspondents before they are due to get funds to loan to the rebel authorities, and now acting Prussian consul here, doing quite as effective service to the rebels as his partner in the field. I find M. Paesher & Co., bankers, whose clerks and employees formed a part of the French Legion, organized to fight the United States, and who contributed largely to arm and equip that corps. These are fair specimens of the *neutrality* of the foreigners, for whom the Government is called upon to interfere to prevent their paying any thing toward the Relief Fund for their starving countrymen.

" If the representatives of the foreign governments will feed their own starving people, — over whom the only protection they extend, so far as I can see, is to tax them all, poor and rich, a dollar and a half each for certificates of nationality, — I will release the foreigners from all the exactions, fines, and imposts whatever.

" I have the honor to be your obedient servant,

"BENJAMIN F. BUTLER,

" *Major-General commanding.*"

A second assessment for the same amount as the first was made on the 9th of December, the first having been exhausted. Further detail or comment were unnecessary. The reader cannot fail to see the justice, as well as the necessity, of the course pursued in this matter by Gen. Butler.

CHAPTER X.

GEN. BUTLER AND THE SECESSIONIST WOMEN OF NEW ORLEANS.

PERHAPS no act of Gen. Butler's life has sub-
jected him to such severe and unjust criticism
as the following order : —

HEADQUARTERS DEPARTMENT OF THE GULF,
NEW ORLEANS, May 15, 1862.

GENERAL ORDER NO. 28:

As the officers and soldiers of the United States have been
subject to repeated insults from the women (calling themselves
ladies) of New Orleans, in return for the most scrupulous non-
interference and courtesy on our part, it is ordered, that hereafter, when any female shall, by word, gesture, or movement,
insult or show contempt for any officer or soldier of the United
States, she shall be regarded and held liable to be treated as a
woman of the town plying her avocation.

By command of

MAJOR-GENERAL BUTLER.

GEORGE C. STRONG, *A. A. G., Chief of Staff.*

The occasion, necessity, and full justification of
this order, was found in the fact that the women of
New Orleans, notably the more aristocratic, adopted
every device possible to feminine ingenuity and spite,
to flaunt their rebel sentiments in the faces of the
officers and soldiers of the United States, and to in-

sult them openly on the street and in the public con-
veyances. They wore rebel flags upon their bonnets.
They would pull their skirts away when passing soldiers, as though to avoid contamination by contact
with them. They would sneer at them, and use insulting epithets, and, in some instances, spit in their
faces on the street. These outrages were not occa-
sional, but constant and almost universal; the officers
and soldiers, on their part, treating all the people well,
and the women with deferential politeness, and taking
no apparent notice of, and in no case resenting, the
insults offered. They chafed under this treatment,
however, and complained daily to the general, of
insults which they as gentlemen could not resent,
nor as sensitive men endure with patience. The
general resolved to protect his men and these women
at the same time, and the above order was the plan
adopted to do it; and the wisdom of it is sustained
by its entire success.

It has been charged, that in this order Gen. Butler
insulted the women of New Orleans, by classing the
whole of them as women of the town; but no just
critic can draw any such conclusion from the language of the document in question. Only those who
should choose to act like women of the town could be
treated as such. How do women of the town act?
Why, they accost men on the street with whom they
have no acquaintance, or they stare at them, or make
signs designed to attract their attention, &c.; and in
all cities of civilized countries women who do such
things are liable to be arrested, committed to prison,
and fined.

No such punishment was meted out to the women of New Orleans under this order, for the excellent reason that from the day of its publication they all comported themselves as became virtuous and well-bred ladies. It was feared by some, even of the general's staff, that the order might be misconstrued by some of the soldiers, who might make it the pretext for insulting women whom they might meet; but no instance of such misunderstanding or abuse of the order occurred. On the contrary, the order produced good fruits only; and, as we are to judge by fruits, we cannot but commend most fully Gen. Butler's celebrated " Woman Order."

It was not popular in rebel circles, either South, North, or in Europe. The mayor of New Orleans was highly indignant. He wrote on the 16th of May a most inflammatory and offensive letter to Gen. Butler, saying, "As chief magistrate of this city I cannot allow such an order published without my protest. The passions of our people already aroused, this must exasperate them beyond control; and I will not undertake to be responsible for the peace of the city while such an edict remains in force."

Gen. Butler took him at his word. He having said he would not be responsible for the order of the city, the following reply was returned : —

"John T. Monroe, late mayor of New Orleans, is hereby relieved from all responsibility for the peace of the city, and suspended from any official functions, and committed to Fort Jackson until further orders.　　B. F. BUTLER,

" *Major-General commanding.*"

The mayor's bravado oozed out at once; and he begged not to be sent to prison, declaring that he had no intention of insulting the general. Gen. Butler explained his order to him, and he professed himself entirely satisfied with it. He at once asked to withdraw his letter; and the general wrote at the foot of it, " This communication having been sent under a mistake of fact, and being improper in language, I desire to apologize for and withdraw it." This the mayor signed, and was relieved from arrest.

The very next day, having been bulldozed by his rebel friends, he wrote to recall his recantation.

In reply Gen. Butler wrote: —

"There can be, there has been, no room for misunderstanding of General Order No. 28. No lady will take any notice of a strange gentleman in such form as to attract attention. Common women do.

"Therefore, whatever woman, lady, or mistress, gentle or simple, who by gesture, look, or word insults, shows contempt for, thus attracting to herself the notice of, my officers or soldiers, will be deemed to act as becomes her vocation of common woman, and will be liable to be treated accordingly.

"I shall not, as I have not abated, a single word of that order: it was well considered. If obeyed, it will protect the true and modest woman from all possible insult: the others will take care of themselves.

"You can publish your letter if you publish this note and your apology.   B. F. BUTLER,
"*Major-General commanding.*"

Again the mayor wilted; and again, under the influence of rebel counsellors, he stiffened up. Finally, on the invitation of Gen. Butler, the mayor and the chief officers of the city had a conference with the general at his office. The general delivered a lecture to them, recounting the broken promises and disloyal conduct of the mayor and council, as well as the leading citizens.

Then addressing them individually he asked, "Do you believe the mayor's letter insulting? Do you aid and abet the mayor? Do you sustain the mayor in reiterating the letter?"

The chief of police, Judge Kennedy, and Mr. Duncan answered in the affirmative. The general then ordered these three gentlemen and the mayor committed to Fort Jackson.

Gen. Butler immediately took control of the city government by proclamation, organizing a police-force, and restoring order.

CHAPTER XI.

THE EXECUTION BY HANGING OF W. B. MUMFORD.

IN the early part of the war Gen. Dix made himself famous by his celebrated order, "If any man pulls down the American flag, shoot him on the spot." The reader remembers the occurrence, already related, of pulling down the flag which Capt. Farragut had ordered raised over the United-States Mint. The man who did this was William B. Mumford, a professional gambler of New Orleans. His act was of treasonable character; but it is not probable he would have been arrested and tried for it if he had afterwards behaved himself in a seemly manner. But he was one of the most troublesome mob-leaders in the city. He was almost daily seen on the street, venting rebel sentiments, and boasting of his exploit in tearing down and insulting the old flag. So bold did he become, that he would repeat the story in front of Gen. Butler's headquarters, and dare the Lincoln hirelings to arrest him. While in the act of repeating this challenge one day, he was arrested, and taken to prison. His case having been thus brought to the special attention of the provost-marshal and provost-judge, he was put on trial; and, being found guilty, he was sentenced to be hung.

During the trial he treated the whole matter with contempt; and after he was condemned he and his friends boldly proclaimed that Gen. Butler would not dare to sign the order for his execution, as it would cost him his life to do so.

They were mistaken in their man. Gen. Butler makes no ostentatious display of his courage, but he is one of the very last to be frightened from the discharge of duty by threats of personal violence.

The general, believing his sentence just, and that his execution would have a healthy influence upon his traitor associates and the whole city, promptly signed his death-warrant, and fixed a day for its execution, naming Saturday, June the 7th.

About this time six men who had broken their parole by joining a secret rebel organization, known as the Monroe Guard, in honor of the mayor, were arrested while in the act of stealing out of the city to join Gen. Lovell's command. These were tried, and condemned to be shot. This sentence the general also indorsed. Hence there were seven men under sentence of death in New Orleans at the same time.

Although he had not acted as judge, hence to sentence them was not his act, yet they could not be put to death without his order; and, even after this had been given, the power to pardon still remained with him.

Gen. Butler is a man of firmness and decision;

but he is also a man of fine sensibilities and tender sympathies, his maligners to the contrary notwithstanding. These seven human lives weighed down his heart to so great an extent that he could neither eat nor sleep with any degree of comfort. To add to his embarrassment, Mumford's wife, his own wife, the venerable and reverend Dr. Mercer, and others, besought him, with prayers and tears, to pardon this wretched man. But he remained firm. Not but that he earnestly desired to grant the pardon; but the public good, aye, the safety of the city, demanded that an example be made of this man. He believed, and still believes, that if Mumford should be pardoned it would be construed as an act of cowardice on his part, and the mob-element Mumford represented would have become uncontrollable save by grape and canister. It was simply a question whether one bad man should meet the fate his crimes deserved, or hundreds, perhaps thousands, should be slain in the streets, the good and the bad together.

The other six men were worthy of death, according to the laws of war; but possibly one victim would suffice. Hence, when a statement came to the general, that one of the poor fellows had said that he did not understand about this paroling, that it was a matter for officers and gentlemen,—"We are not officers nor gentlemen,"—he promptly commuted their sentence to imprisonment on Ship Island during the pleasure of the President. He was doubtless influenced toward this action by the earnest petition of Hon. T. J. Durant, then a prominent citizen of New

Orleans, a pronounced Union-man, and now a distin-guished member of the bar at Washington City, and others of influence; but the matter that touched his heart in its most tender place was the words of the poor fellow who unconsciously drew such a sharp distinction between the intelligent traitors and their deluded victims, the common rebel soldiers.

Mumford was hung on the 7th of June, in the presence of an immense crowd; and the city felt safer from that hour.

Gen. Butler had received numerous letters threat-ening him with assassination unless he pardoned Mumford; but no attempt of the sort occurred. On the contrary, his life was much safer after than before the execution.

· CHAPTER XII.

GEN. BUTLER IN THE RÔLE OF A DIPLOMAT. — HE
PROVES MORE THAN A MATCH FOR THE FOREIGN
CONSULS.

BEING a great commercial city, New Orleans was
honored with the permanent presence of consul-
generals from the leading nations of the world; and
during the war these, without exception, sympathized
with the rebel cause, and most if not all of them had
taken the oath of allegiance to the Southern Confederacy in 1861. This act of theirs was without
excuse; they being foreigners, and accredited representatives of their respective governments to the
Government of the United States. Being in sympathy with the rebels, they opposed every measure of
Gen. Butler; and, being foreign officials, they claimed
exemption from the rules and laws governing citizens: hence they were a very troublesome set of fellows.

There was a large foreign population in the city;
and these consuls assumed the duty of protecting
these also from the action of such laws as Gen.
Butler ordained for the government of the city.

Had the commanding general been free to act without fear of interference from the State Department, he could have managed these obstreperous and officious officials without much difficulty; but they were constantly appealing to their ministers at Washington, who in turn laid their grievances before Secretary Seward, who, it is well known, was nothing if not a diplomat, — a suave and genial, not to say timid, diplomat, with not one element of the soldier in his make-up.

Gen. Butler is both a diplomat and a general, a statesman and a soldier. He understood the rights and duties of these foreign consuls, and respected them; and he also understood the rights of his own Government, and was resolved to maintain them against domestic foes and foreign enemies.

An organization known as the British Guard, composed of wealthy Englishmen, sent their arms and equipments to Gen. Beauregard; on learning which fact, Gen. Butler ordered them to leave the city within twenty-four hours, on pain of imprisonment in Fort Jackson as dangerous foes.

The British consul, Mr. Coppell, protested.

The general replied, that, as they had thought it important that Gen. Beauregard should have sixty more uniforms and guns, he preferred that he should have these faithless and dangerous men, to their remaining in the city as a disturbing element. He therefore stood by his order; and with the exception of the captain and one man, who were sent to prison, the legion fled the city.

A Frenchman by the name of Heidsick, disguised
as a bar-tender, carried despatches between the rebels
in the city and the rebel commander at Mobile, on
the steamer "Dick Keys," which Gen. Butler had
permitted to bring provisions to the city. For this
he was arrested, and sent to prison. The French
consul protested ; and, finding Gen. Butler firm, he
laid the matter before Secretary Seward, through the
French minister, who had him released, instead of
letting him be tried as a spy, and hung, as he richly
deserved.

The Citizens' Bank had transferred eight hundred
thousand dollars in silver to the office of the Dutch
consul on the surrender of the city ; and, on learning
of this fact, Gen. Butler seized it with the purpose of
holding it, and thus preventing it from being conveyed to the rebel authorities.

Another sum of over seven hundred thousand
dollars was found in possession of a liquor-dealer, a
Frenchman by the name of Couterrie, and also
seized and held for the same reason. The evident
object in both these cases was to put this coin, which
belonged to rebel corporations, into the custody of
foreign consuls for protection until it could safely be
shipped to the Confederate authorities. It was therefore properly confiscate, but Gen. Butler only put it
in a safe place subject to the orders of his Government. The Dutch and French consuls protested,
and Reverdy Johnson was sent to New Orleans to
investigate the matter. The result was that Mr.
Johnson turned a willing ear to the rebel bankers

and other interested parties, and a deaf ear to Gen.
Butler; and this immense sum of fifteen hundred
thousand dollars was turned over to the enemies of
the Government, and ultimately found its way into
the Confederate treasury, and was used to pay for
foreign arms and equipments with which to fight the
Government of the United States.

Mr. Johnson decided various other cases, brought
before him by rebel merchants and others, and all in
their favor; and all these decisions were made
against the earnest protest of Gen. Butler, sustained
by well-established facts and legal arguments, overwhelmingly convincing to a mind free from prejudice.

Among the remarkable facts connected with Gen.
Butler's career at New Orleans, none testify to his
greatness, his wisdom in planning, and his energy in
execution, more prominently than the fact that not a
case of yellow-fever occurred in the city during the
season of 1862. This fearful disease raged in Nassau,
Havana, and other neighboring ports; but although
New Orleans had formerly been one of its favorite
haunts, and notwithstanding the fact that the city
had twenty thousand unacclimated people in it, it
did not lose a life from yellow-fever during the time
Gen. Butler was in command. This wonderful exemption from the fell pestilence was due to his
successful efforts to have the city cleaned, and his
excellent quarantine, which prevented both the spon-
taneous generation and the importation of the dis-
ease-germs.

The foes of the general and of the Government predicted that the yellow-fever would relieve them of his presence, and of the presence of a large portion of the Northern troops, before the summer should close : hence they were indignant at his determined purpose and successful efforts to ward it off. The foreign consuls complained of his strict quarantine system, and laid their complaints before the Secretary of State. Gen. Butler replied in his characteristically able and vigorous manner, defending himself most perfectly by facts that were incontrovertible. He closed by saying, —

"Allow me to repeat, that with the blessing of God, to whom our most devout thanks are duly due for his goodness, the fell scourge, the yellow-fever, has been kept from my command and the city of New Orleans, till now, when all danger is past, by the firm administration of sanitary and quarantine regulations, in spite of complaints and difficulties; and, if my acts need it, I point to the results as an unanswerable vindication."

CHAPTER XIII.

GEN. BUTLER MAKES AN EFFORT TO RESTORE CONFIDENCE AND PROSPERITY THROUGHOUT THE STATE.

GEN. BUTLER is a strict constructionist. He believes with all his heart in the strictest obedience to law. In times of peace, the common and civil law are his sufficient guides : in a state of war, the rules of war and the orders of his superiors govern his actions. He found himself, however, now in an anomalous position ; and he felt at liberty to act upon his own judgment, and the dictates of common sense, humanity, and patriotism. He was engaged in putting down an insurrection, not fighting a foreign foe. He believed that so soon as the leaders of the Rebellion should be vanquished or captured, the people would see the folly and sin of secession, and return to their loyalty to the Government which had so justly and benignly protected their rights, and fostered their interests. Holding these views, and having conquered New Orleans and a good portion of Louisiana, he not only resolved upon such measures as he deemed necessary to the maintenance of the authority of the United States over any who might be still rebelliously disposed, but to restore as far as possible the conditions of peace and the elements of prosperity.

On the 4th of May, 1862, he issued the following address to the people : —

"The commanding general of the department having been informed that rebellious, lying, and desperate men have represented, and are now representing, to the honest planters and good people of the State of Louisiana, that the United-States Government, by its forces, have come here to confiscate and destroy their crop of cotton and sugar, it is hereby ordered to be made known by publication in all the newspapers of this city, that all cargoes of cotton and sugar shall have safe conduct of the forces of the United States; and the boats bringing them from beyond the lines of the United-States forces may be allowed to return in safety, after a reasonable delay, if their owners so desire, provided they bring no passengers except the owners and managers of said boats and of the property so conveyed, and no other merchandise except provisions, of which such boats are requested to bring a full supply, for the benefit of the poor of this city."

He not only authorized all merchants and other tradesmen of the city to re-open their places of business, and continue to carry on their regular trade ; but those who refused were compelled to do so, on penalty of fine. The currency of the city was in a bad condition; the banks having suspended specie-payments six months or more before, and adopted the Confederate currency as the only circulating medium except shinplasters issued by tradesmen, car-tickets, &c.

The capture of the city sent Confederate notes

down seventy per cent; but, as they constituted the
bulk of the currency, they continued to circulate by
permission of Gen. Butler, and the consent of the
people, for some weeks.   It was his fixed purpose,
however, to reconstruct the financial system as soon
as it could be done without violence or injustice.
The banks had suspended specie-payment, and also
stopped emitting their own bills, in September, 1861,
and had sent a large part of their gold and silver
coin to the secretary of the rebel treasury, who furnished Confederate currency instead.   Gen. Butler,
on learning these facts, resolved that these banks
should restore to the people the same currency, gold,
silver, and bank-notes, formerly in use ; and as the
worthless Confederate notes had been forced upon
the people, in place of their former currency, by the
banks, he thought it but just, that whatever loss
might occur, the banks, and not the people, should
sustain ; and on the 16th of May he issued the following order : —

"I. It is hereby ordered that neither the city of New Orleans,
nor the banks thereof, exchange their notes, bills, or obligations
for Confederate notes, bills, or bonds, nor issue any bill, note,
or obligation payable in Confederate notes.

"II. On the twenty-seventh day of May inst., all circulation
of, or trade in, Confederate notes and bills will cease within this
department; and all sales or transfers of property made on or
after that day, in consideration of such notes or bills, directly
or indirectly, will be void, and the property confiscated to the
United States, one-fourth thereof to go to the informer.

"B. F. BUTLER."

This threw the bankers into a panic ; and they

resolved to unload their Confederate currency before the 27th, thus throwing the loss involved by their own former action upon the innocent people.

The papers of the next day contained announcements from the various banks, of which the following is a sample : —

"All persons having deposited Confederate notes in this banking-house are notified to withdraw them before the 27th inst. Such balances as may not be withdrawn will be considered at the risk of the owners."

As Mr. Parton, in his "Butler in New Orleans," justly says, —

"The banks had introduced this worthless currency, had grown rich upon it, and now determined to throw its loss upon their innocent victims, — the people. What rendered the course of the banks the more exasperating was the fact, that a wealthy corporation, professing entire faith in the ultimate triumph of the Confederacy, could afford to hold its paper, while a poor trader would be ruined by the suspension of his little capital."

Gen. Butler read these advertisements as he sipped his coffee on the morning they appeared, and immediately wrote the following : —

NEW ORLEANS, May 19, 1862.

GENERAL ORDER No. 30:

It is represented to the commanding general that great distress, privation, hunger, and even starvation, have been brought upon the people of New Orleans and vicinage by the course taken by the banks and dealers in currency.

He has been urged to take measures to provide, as far as may be, for the relief of the citizens, so that the loss may fall, at least, on those who have caused and ought to bear it.

The general sees with regret that the banks and bankers

causelessly suspended specie-payments in September last, in contravention of the laws of the State and of the United States.

Having done so, they introduced Confederate notes as currency, which they bought at a discount, in place of their own bills, receiving them on deposit, paying them out for their discounts, and collecting their customers' notes and drafts in them as money, sometimes even against their will, thus giving these notes credit and a wide general circulation; so that they were substituted in the hands of the middling-men, the poor and unwary, as currency, in place of that provided by the Constitution and laws of the country, or of any valuable equivalent.

The banks and bankers now endeavor to take advantage of the re-establishment of the authority of the United States to throw the depreciation and loss from this worthless stuff of their creation and fostering upon their creditors, depositors, and bill-holders.

They refuse to receive these bills, while they pay them over their counters.

They require their depositors to take them.

They change the obligation of contracts by stamping their bills, "Redeemable in Confederate notes."

They have invested the savings of labor and the pittance of the widow in this paper.

They sent away or hid their specie, so that the people could have nothing but these notes, which they now depreciate, with which to buy bread.

All other property has become nearly valueless from the calamities of this iniquitous and unjust war begun by rebellious guns turned on the flag of our prosperous and happy country floating over Fort Sumter. Saved from the general ruin by a system of financiering, bank-stocks alone are now selling at great premiums in the market, while the stockholders have received large dividends.

To equalize, as far as may be, this general loss; to have it fall, at least in part, where it ought to lie; to enable the people of this city and vicinage to have a currency which shall at least be a semblance to that which the wisdom of the Constitution provides for all citizens of the United States, — it is therefore

Ordered, I. That the several incorporated banks pay out no more Confederate notes to their depositors or creditors ; but that all depositors be paid in the bills of the bank, United States treasury notes, gold, or silver.

II. That all private bankers receiving deposits pay out to their depositors only the current bills of the city banks, or United-States treasury notes, gold, or silver.

III. That the savings banks pay to their depositors or creditors only gold, silver, or United-States treasury notes, current bills of city banks, or their own bills, to an amount not exceeding one-third of their deposits, and of denomination not less than one dollar, which they are authorized to issue, and for the redemption of which their assets shall be held liable.

IV. The incorporated banks are authorized to issue bills of a less denomination than five dollars, but not less than one dollar, any thing in their charters to the contrary notwithstanding; and are authorized to receive Confederate notes for any of their bills until the twenty-seventh day of May inst.

V. That all persons and firms having issued small notes, or "shinplasters" so called, are required to redeem them on presentation at their places of business, between the hours of nine A.M. and three P.M., either in gold, silver, United-States treasury notes, or current bills of city banks, under penalty of confiscation of their property, and sale thereof, for the purpose of redemption of the notes so issued, or imprisonment for a term at hard labor.

VI. Private bankers may issue notes of denominations not less than one dollar, nor more than ten dollars, to two-thirds of the amount of specie which they show to a commissioner appointed from these headquarters, in their vaults, actually kept there for the purpose of redemption of such notes.

Mr. Parton tells us that "The relief afforded by the publication of this order was such that, as a

secessionist remarked to a member of the general's
staff, it was equivalent to a re-enforcement of twenty
thousand men to the Union army; and Union men
say that nothing but the continual bad news from
McClellan's army prevented this measure from caus-
ing an open and general manifestation of Union feeling. But as it was thought probable that the city
would again, and soon, pass into the hands of the
rebels, the people feared to commit themselves to a
course that would invite the vengeance of the returning Confederates."

One bank protested, but, the general remaining
firm, it was obliged to submit with the best grace it
could; and in a very short period the city had as
sound a currency as New York or Boston, and commerce revived at once, — a remarkable illustration of
Gen. Butler's financial ability. It is said that the
bankers of New Orleans expressed great surprise at
finding a Yankee lawyer and volunteer general as
much at home in the domain of finance as if he had
spent his whole life in a bank. Having restored a
sound currency, the general turned his great powers
of intellect in favor of a general restoration of the
commerce of the city and the agriculture of the
State. He had brought his army to New Orleans on
board of chartered transport-ships. These he must
return in ballast; and to ballast with sand from Ship
Island would cost a large sum. For example: the
steamer "Mississippi" cost the Government fifteen
hundred dollars per day; to bring two hundred and
fifty tons of sand in small boats, and load it in, would

take ten days, and to discharge it in New York, four more : fourteen days, at fifteen hundred dollars per day, is twenty-one thousand dollars. He could ballast with sugar, and make a large profit, and besides increase the revenues of the merchants of New Orleans and the planters of Louisiana, as well as of the United States. A brilliant idea!

He had very little government money; so he pledged his private credit for a hundred thousand dollars, and loaned it to the Government to buy sugar with which to load these ships. This transaction was very profitable to the Government; while all Gen. Butler received in the way of reward was a large dividend of abuse and slander, which grew out of the fact that other people judged him by themselves. The owners of the ships, though receiving enormous rental for their vessels, insisted on being paid freights on this sugar, which the general justly refused; and, failing in their efforts to rob the Government, through the integrity of Gen. Butler, who opposed their claims, they accused him, by insinuation and hint only, of making money on this sugar operation. It is possible they thought that in some way he was re-imbursed for the use of his money; but the Secretary of the Treasury knew he did not make a dollar. It has been stated as a fact by half the newspapers of the country, and repeated by his political opponents thousands of times, that Gen. Butler got rich while in New Orleans, by speculating in sugar and cotton. The author, after thorough investigation, is prepared to state positively, and does so state, that

the charge is *absolutely false* in every part and par-
ticular. Not that these editors and politicians, and
even preachers, all mean to be guilty of wilful lying.
Some of them do ; but they gladly believe a lie which
sounds reasonable, and suits their purpose, — that of
injuring the man they envy or fear. Gen. Butler's
only cotton transaction was as follows : —

"The navy captured a small schooner laden with cotton.
'I needed,' says the general, 'the schooner as a lighter, and
took her from the navy. What should be done with the cotton?
A transport was going home empty : it would cost nothing
to transport it. To whom should I send it? To my quartermaster at Boston? But I supposed him on the way here.
Owing to the delays of the expedition, I found all the quarter-
masters, men, and artisans on the island, whose services were
indispensable, almost in a state of mutiny for want of pay.
There was not a dollar of government funds on the island. I
had but seventy-five dollars of my own. The sutler had money
he would loan on my draft on my private banker. I borrowed
on such draft about four thousand dollars, quite equal to the
value of the cotton, as I received it; and with the money I
paid the government debts to the laborers, so that their wives
and children would not starve. In order that my draft should
be paid, I sent the cotton to my correspondent at Boston, with
directions to sell it, pay my draft out of the proceeds, and hold
the rest, if any, subject to my order, so that, upon the account
stated, I might settle with the Government. What was done?
The Government seized the cotton, without a word of explana-
tion to me, kept it until it had depreciated ten per cent, and
allowed my draft to be dishonored; and it had to be paid out
of the little fund I had left at home for the support of my children in my absence."

When the history of the cotton, and of the transactions connected with it, reached the Government,

the money Gen. Butler had spent was refunded to him, with an apology for the bad treatment he had received.

It will be seen that the sole object in both transactions was to serve the Government, and promote the interests of others, — the planters in the one case, and the employees in the other ; and these were the only instances of his having any connection with such matters.

It was to be expected that secessionists and secession organs, North and South, would denounce and slander an officer so able and active as Gen. Butler ; and they did. His taking possession of and occupying the residence of Gen. Twiggs furnished an excuse for starting on its rounds the now notorious but absurd story that he stole the spoons and other articles of silver plate which he found there. The author asked Gen. Butler for a statement in regard to the plate found in the Twiggs mansion. He said, —

"On moving into the residence of Gen. Twiggs I found no plate ; but a few days later one of the general's former servants informed me that a box of valuables was buried beneath the floor of a cellar. This I ordered dug up. I found with this box three elegant swords which had been presented to Gen. Twiggs in recognition of his public services in the Mexican war, with a lot of silver plate. The swords I forwarded to the President, with a recommendation that one of them be hung in the Patent Office, one in West Point Academy, and the other be presented to some officer of the army for distinguished services.

"The President adopted my recommendation, and laid it before Congress, where it rests still. The swords were still at the White House after Mr. Johnson became President; but at my request I was permitted to deposit them in a treasury-vault for safe keeping. The silver plate I ordered put back on to the sideboard; and during my residence there I used it as I did other ware and furniture; and on surrendering the command to my successor, Gen. Banks, I turned it over to him, taking the receipt of his quartermaster for it. I hear that it subsequently disappeared in some mysterious way, but I have no means of knowing who got it. Some time after the war a daughter of Gen. Twiggs called upon me in Washington, accompanied by Gen. Garfield, to inquire as to the disposal of her father's swords. I told her that the swords were in one of the vaults of the Treasury Building; that there were two keys to the box containing them, one of which was in the possession of the Secretary of the Treasury, and the other in my possession. Seeing no reason why she should not now have these swords, I gave her a letter to the Secretary, recommending that they be returned to the family through her. It was not done, however; and the swords are still where I deposited them, in the treasury. I said to Miss Twiggs, 'Why don't you ask about the family plate? I suppose you think I took that, and I don't blame you for thinking so; but I am glad of this opportunity to relieve myself from that suspicion.' I then told her of the voucher of Gen. Banks, covering, among other things, this lost plate. That [said the general] is all I know about the spoon story, except that it was started in the Virginia legislature by one Daniels, whom I had punished for subornation of perjury, a secessionist member of that body, who was afterwards appointed by Johnson to a customs office in Norfolk, defaulted, and ran away."

Gen. Butler could not revive the trade of New Orleans with the interior of the State very greatly, for the reason, that, acting on the advice of fiery rebel leaders, the planters had destroyed most of their cotton to prevent its falling into the general's hands.

But his efforts proved his good intentions, and had great influence in restoring confidence in and respect for the Government he represented; and all seemed going well, till the news of the disasters to our forces in Virginia raised the hopes of the rebels that it would be but a short time before New Orleans would again be under Confederate rule. As this impression strengthened under the influence of the continued bad news from Washington and Richmond, the mob element again asserted itself. On the 10th of July an alarming riot occurred. A woman not only displayed a secession badge on the street near the general's headquarters, but used insulting language toward a soldier, evidently for the purpose of provoking an attempt to arrest her; and when a policeman took her in charge, she appealed to the Southern chivalry for protection, in a manner so dramatic, that an attack was at once made upon the officer by the mob. Clubs were used freely, and a pistol was fired. The policeman was knocked down, and a soldier wounded. A military officer fired on the assassin who shot the soldier, when at least one hundred returned rebel soldiers joined the mob; and, but for the courage and firmness of the police and Union soldiers present, a terrible tragedy would undoubtedly have occurred, and the riot would have become general throughout the city, which was evidently the purpose of this woman and her allies. She and some of her chief supporters were taken before Gen. Shepley, who sent her to Gen. Butler. The general recognized her as the wife, or mistress, of a notorious gambler, then in Fort Jackson for a similar offence; and he sent her there to keep him company.

A few days subsequently, the funeral procession accompanying the body of the gallant Lieut. De Kay was insulted by rebel women; and Mrs. Philips, wife of Philip Philips, well known at Washington as a prominent favorite at the White House during Buchanan's administration, and who had been banished from the capital for aiding the rebels early in the war, was arrested and imprisoned. She was released after a few weeks, by order of Gen. Butler, on her promise to behave herself in a proper manner henceforth.

But to record all the incidents connected with Gen. Butler's career at New Orleans would require many volumes: a few only can be given in this brief history, enough to show that his rule was vigorous, humane, patriotic, just, and wise, hence successful.

That the mailed hand of this great chieftain rested upon Southern men and women with such fearful power, was due to the fact that they were in rebellion against the Government, and he was putting down rebellion. He did not spare his own men when they violated the law, as the following incident clearly shows.

Complaints reached the general on the 12th of June, that a party of men, bearing a pretended order from him, had robbed a house on Toulouse Street, which they had entered under pretence of searching for concealed arms. He took prompt measures for their detection and arrest; and on the same day four

men were arrested, and brought before him. He
had an indistinct recollection of one of them, and
asked, "Where have I seen you?"

"In Boston."

"Where in Boston?"

"In the municipal court."

"For what offence were you before that court?"

"Burglary."

"What regiment did you join?"

"The Thirtieth Massachusetts."

"Why are you not with your regiment?"

"I was discharged."

"What for?"

"Disease."

"Well, you ought to be hanged; for you have
robbed before, and been convicted."

"*Don't* do it, general, and I'll tell you all about it."

He said he was a member of a band organized
for plundering houses. Two others confessed their
guilt, and three further arrests were made on the
next day. After a fair trial, Lieut. William M. Clary,
late second officer of the United-States steam transport "Saxon," Stanislaus Roy of New Orleans,
George William Craig, late first officer of "The City
of New York," Frank Newton, late private of the
Thirteenth Connecticut Volunteers, and Theodore
Lieb of New Orleans, were convicted; and on the
16th of June, Craig, Newton, Clary, and Roy were
hung; while Lieb, in consequence of his extreme
youth, he being but eighteen, was sent to prison
during the pleasure of the President.

" The effect of this," says Mr. Parton, " was most salutary upon the minds of both parties in New Orleans." It settled the fact that Gen. Butler was a just man, who would protect the righteous, and punish the iniquitous, whether friend or foe, as the terms were then understood; though Gen. Butler knew no foes but those in open rebellion against the Government, nor friends save those who obeyed its just laws.

CHAPTER XIV.

TAKING THE OATH OF ALLEGIANCE. — THE PEOPLE OF
NEW ORLEANS REQUIRED TO DEFINE THEIR POSI-
TION. — MORE TROUBLE WITH THE CONSULS, ETC.

ON the 10th of June, Gen. Butler issued General
Order No. 41, requiring all civil officers and
attorneys to take the oath of allegiance as a condition
precedent to their continuing to exercise their respective functions. All citizens who might desire to
receive the protection of the Government (except
mere protection from personal violence), or any favor,
privilege, passport, &c., or to have money paid them,
or property delivered to them, must take the oath of
allegiance.

All foreigners claiming protection or favors from
the United States were required to swear to do no
act, or conceal, or consent to any act that should aid
or comfort, any of the enemies or opposers of the
United States, while their respective governments
remained at peace with the United States.

This order aroused the ire of the foreign consuls,
as well as the domestic traitors. "The Delta" hu-
morously said, —

" If Gen. Butler rides up street, the consuls are sure to come
in a body, and protest that he did not ride down.   If he smokes
a pipe in the morning, a deputation calls upon him in the evening to know why he did not smoke a cigar.   If he drinks coffee,
they will send some rude messenger with a note asking in the
name of some tottering dynasty why he did not drink tea."

In this instance they joined in a lengthy protest,
which wholly misrepresented the order, and was evidently meant to mislead the people, and prejudice
them against Gen. Butler, rather than to right any
wrong possible to those they professed to represent.

The general replied, reviewing in a most scathing
manner the treasonable record of the consuls and
other foreigners, showing that many had joined the
rebel army, and all had willingly sworn allegiance to
the Confederate Government: hence he could not
abate his order, to oblige even so respectable and
sensitive a body of gentlemen as the seven representatives of European states, whose names were signed
to the protest.

The aristocracy of New Orleans protested, not in
a formal, but a most effectual way.   Persons who
took the oath were denied admission to the best
society.   Gentlemen were cut on the street by ladies
of their acquaintance, and turned out of boarding-
houses by high-toned landladies.   The advantages
were so great, however, that a very large number
took the oath, over fourteen thousand within a month.
With a view to the absolute preservation of the city
from riot and bloodshed, the general ordered all private arms, revolvers, bowie-knives, &c., to be sur-

rendered to the military authorities. Of course the consuls protested; but the city was completely disarmed, notwithstanding this official protest, every man receiving a receipt for his property, with assurance of its return so soon as the interests of the city and country would justify it.

The complaint, that disarming the people would subject them to danger of being robbed, caused the general to issue the following order: —

"That, hereafter, the offences of robbery by violence or aggravated assault, that ought to be repelled by the use of deadly weapons, burglaries, rapes, and murders, whether committed by blacks or whites, will be, on conviction, punished by death."

Following upon the order to take the oath of allegiance, and the disarming of the city, came the one to confiscate the property of rebellious citizens.

This was in direct obedience to the act of Congress of July 17, 1862, which made it the duty of all commanding generals to confiscate to the use of the Government at once all property of all who held office, civil or military, under the Confederate Government, and of all others who refused to take the oath of allegiance to the United States within sixty days after notice by proclamation by the President.

Among the leading traitors of New Orleans, Gen. Twiggs and John Slidell were most prominent, and their estates were the first which Gen. Butler seized; and the aristocratic mansion of the former became the residence of the commanding general and his staff. Among the papers of Gen. Twiggs were found letters which proved that he had sought the command of the Union forces in Texas for the express purpose of betraying his Government, — an act only paralleled by the treason of Benedict Arnold. Gen. Butler found that constant vigilance was necessary to defeat the ingenuity and activity of the rebel people of New Orleans. Those who were allowed sixty days' grace before the confiscation-act could reach their property began at once to dispose of it by sale at nominal prices to non-residents, minors, &c. The general met this with an order rendering all such transfers illegal and null. He was resolved that nothing should save their property from confiscation but the taking of the oath of allegiance.

The clergy of the city were all rebels in sentiment, and resolved to remain so: yet they hoped to escape the loss of their property on account of their sacred profession, — surely no profane hand could ruthlessly touch the money or property of a minister of the gospel. Rev. Dr. Mercer wrote Gen. Butler, claiming to be entirely neutral, but refusing to take the oath. The general replied, —

"In my opinion, there can be no such thing as neutrality by a citizen of the United States. He that is not for us is against us. As an officer, I cannot recognize such neutrality. All good citizens are called upon to lend their influence to the United States: all who do not do so are the enemies of the United States. I cannot permit any reservation of property from the list, or any exemption of persons from the requirements of Order No. 76."

Rev. Dr. Leacock claimed to be a Union-man, yet declined to take the oath; but Gen. Butler had got possession of a sermon of his, preached in November, 1860, and published as a campaign document by the leaders of the secession movement. This sermon was full of rebel sentiment. It closed as follows : —

"I am willing, at the call of my country, to die a free man; but I'll never, no, never, live a slave; and the alternative now presented by our enemies is *secession* or slavery. Let it be liberty or death!"

The reverend doctor did not succeed in softening the heart of the general so far as to secure exemption from the order.

Major Strong, chief of Gen. Butler's staff, being a good Episcopalian, went into Rev. Dr. Goodrich's church on an October sabbath, and joined the exercises until the prayer for the President was reached, which was omitted, the doctor asking the congregation to spend a few moments in silent prayer. There could be but one reason for this, — to pray in silence for Jefferson Davis.

The major was indignant; and, rising to his feet, he said, "Stop, sir! It is my duty to bring these exercises to a close. I came here for the sole purpose of worshipping God; but, as you omit invoking the blessing our church-service requires upon the President of the nation, I propose to close the services. This house will be shut within ten minutes."

The minister was full of holy (?) wrath, the ladies indignant; but the major's orders were obeyed.

Gen. Butler summoned the Episcopal clergy to meet him at his office on the next day. They claimed that they were only obeying the orders of their bishop, the Right Rev. Major-Gen. Polk. The general refused to recognize the authority.

Dr. Leacock asked, "Well, general, are you going to shut up the churches?"

"No, sir. I am more likely to shut up the ministers." And he did, filling their places by chaplains from his army.

Major Strong and Dr. Goodrich subsequently met in New York, and had a pleasant time talking and laughing over their first meeting. The good doctor had got pretty thoroughly reconstructed in the mean time, — a fine illustration of the flexibility of the human mind, which at one time, owing solely to the prejudices of education and the circumstances surrounding it, honestly holds to views which at another it with equal sincerity repudiates. In this fact is found the hope we all entertain of perfect restoration of that fraternal feeling and bond of national unity between the people of this country which characterized our fathers in the early days of the Republic.

CHAPTER XV.

GEN. BUTLER DEALING WITH THE NEGRO-QUESTION.
— GEN. PHELPS THINKS HIM AN OLD HUNKER ON
THE SUBJECT, AND RESIGNS. — PRESIDENT LINCOLN'S
PRIVATE ORDERS TO GEN. BUTLER, THE SECRET OF
HIS POLICY, ETC.

WHEN Gen. Butler was about leaving Washington for New Orleans, President Lincoln said to him, "The Government is not yet ready to announce a negro policy. We hope to arrive at one ere long. In the mean time, endeavor to avoid raising insoluble problems and sharply defined issues. Try to manage so that neither abolitionists nor conservatives will have room to find fault." Rather difficult instructions to follow under the circumstances surrounding Gen. Butler; but he followed them as nearly as possible.

The negroes everywhere seemed to regard the soldiers as their friends; and they only waited for the smallest hint to rush in, and claim the protection of the army. Indeed, it was a difficult task to keep them out of the lines. In many cases it would have been not only unjust and cruel to have done so, but impolitic, for the reason that they brought valuable information which could be relied upon. The slaves were all loyal to the Government; but the army could not feed, or find employment for, an army of one hundred thousand black men, women, and children, nor would it have been the proper thing to do, to take them off the plantations while the crops were in process of cultivation. Had Gen. Butler had full discretionary power, he would have solved the problem by issuing a proclamation of emancipation, including a provision binding the negroes to remain with their former masters on such wages as could afterwards be agreed upon; but he dared not risk a revocation of such an order, after the news of the fate of Gen. Hunter's emancipation proclamation in South Carolina.

In New Orleans negroes were given the same protection the whites received, even to the extent of being permitted to testify in courts of justice: hence cruelty to slaves substantially ceased in the city, for the reason that if a negro was whipped, or in any manner ill-treated, he or she could have the master or mistress arrested, and Major Bell tried such cases just as he would if such relations as slave and master had not existed.

Gen. Butler gave orders which were to be considered permanent, to admit all colored persons who might ask to see him: his chief reason for which order was that he had a voluntary, vigilant, and trustworthy spy in every negro in his department, and this because the negroes knew that in the general they had a friend who would redress their wrongs.

Gen. J. W. Phelps, an old-time Vermont abolition- ist, a man of honest purpose and strong convictions, was in command of the post at Carrollton. To his camp the poor slaves came singly and in gangs. He welcomed them, and resolved, if not interfered with, to turn all the able-bodied men into soldiers.

Complaints began to come to Gen. Butler, that Gen. Phelps was harboring slaves of Union men; and the general, fearing that if not checked, this influx of negroes would overwhelm Gen. Phelps, wrote him to not permit unemployed persons, black or white, to come into his lines, or remain there. Gen. Phelps felt injured and grieved, and at once wrote a labored protest, covering in his argument the whole question. This was not only meant for the eye of his superior officer, but for that of the President, to whom he asked that it be sent.

Gen. Butler forwarded this able letter, accompany- ing it by one of his own, in which he said, —

"Gen. Phelps, I believe, intends making this a test case for the policy of the Government. I wish it might be so, for the difference of our action upon this subject is a source of trouble. I respect his honest sincerity of opinion; but I am a soldier, bound to carry out the wishes of my Government so long as I hold its commission, and I understand that policy to be the one I am pursuing. I beg to leave the whole matter with the President, with the assurance that his wishes shall be loyally followed."

No reply coming for a month, Gen. Phelps took it for granted that his views were indorsed; and he at once organized three regiments of colored troops, making a requisition for arms and clothing, &c., on

Capt. Davis, A.A.G., New Orleans. Gen. Butler had just received authority to employ as many negro laborers as the service might require; and he ordered Gen. Phelps to put his negroes to work cutting down trees, and forming abattis, and instructed the quartermaster to furnish axes, tents, &c.

Gen. Phelps refused to do this, and insisted upon his own plan of making soldiers of the negroes. Gen. Butler was patient but firm. A long correspondence ensued; and finally Gen. Phelps, finding he could not have his own way in the matter, resigned, and left the service. He returned to his farm in the Green Mountain State, where the offer of a major-general's commission reached him a year later; but he declined it on the ground that it did not date back to the time of his resignation, so as to be an indorsement of his position at that time.

ARMING THE FREE COLORED MEN.

After the battle of Baton Rouge, Gen. Butler resolved to arm the free colored men of New Orleans, in doing which he was but following the example of Gen. Jackson when in command of the city, during the war of 1812. This measure seemed a necessity; for, although the rebel forces were being re-enforced all about him, his urgent requests for additional troops had been refused by the authorities at Washington, on the ground that they could not spare them.

On consultation with some of the principal colored men, the general found them eager to enter the ranks of the army of freedom; and in a short time three regiments of infantry, and two companies of artillery, were ready for duty. There were very few full-blooded negroes, or mulattoes even, among them: they were quadroons and octoroons, in whose veins ran the best blood of Louisiana, and they did not disgrace it on the battle-field.

This measure of Gen. Butler's met the approval of the Union citizens of the city, as well as most of his officers and men; but the secessionists of course objected, although the rebel governor, Moore, had armed these same men in the interest of secession in 1861.

A mob of Frenchmen came in collision with a detachment of colored troops, whom they attacked on the street, the result of which was that the Frenchmen got worsted, of which the French consul complained to the commanding general, and was answered that these men had as good blood in them, indeed, the same that warmed the heart of the distinguished French author Alexandre Dumas, who was treated with the utmost respect by the aristocracy of Paris: and, besides, his countrymen had been entirely to blame in this affair; the colored troops had simply defended themselves when attacked by an unlawful and brutal mob.

About the middle of October, Gen. Butler resolved to put the fugitive and contraband negroes to work on the plantations that had been abandoned by their owners. His plan was to work these plantations on behalf of the Government, paying the negroes living wages. This or some other plan for the relief of these poor creatures was a necessity if he would not see them starve; for there were many thousands of them without masters, homes, or food.

The general also resolved to give the loyal planters of Louisiana an opportunity to try the experiment of the wage-system with the negroes; and this resolution was put in the form of a general order on the 18th of October. Both plans worked admirably.

On being informed by letter from Gen. Butler, of these radical innovations, President Lincoln seemed much interested and pleased. It will interest the reader to learn that the first barrel of sugar made by the negroes of Louisiana under this new system of paid labor was sent to the President of the United States, accompanied by a letter from Gen. Butler in which he says, "The fact that it will have no flavor of the cruel and degrading whip will not, I know, render it less sweet to your taste."

Never, perhaps, in the history of the world, did it devolve on one man to decide so many new questions, and establish so many precedents, under such embarrassing circumstances, in so brief a period, as fell to the lot of Gen. Butler during his career as commander of the Department of the Gulf; and surely never were such generalship, statesmanship, and executive wisdom displayed as characterized his administration. The history of it reads like a romance; and, if it had come down to us from the days of Julius Cæsar, we would regard it as extravagant fiction instead of reliable chronicle. Doubtless future generations will find it impossible to fully credit it. The history of a single day at Gen. Butler's headquarters will give some definite idea of the amount of work and the variety and multiplicity of duties which pressed upon him.

We quote from Parton's " Butler in New Orleans : "

" From eight to nine he received at his residence ladies who had business with him. At nine he drove to his office, where six mounted orderlies and as many clerks awaited his orders; and from one to two hundred people were assembled in the ante-room, anxious to give information, make complaints, or ask favors. Being seated in his chair, beside a broad table on which lay a pistol within easy reach, to protect himself from assassination, which was constantly threatened, the heads of departments were admitted. Then the Relief Commission and the Labor Commission. Next foreign consuls, bank-directors, and other persons of importance. Then the public were admitted, thirty at a time, and ranged in a semicircle before him. Beginning at one end of the line, he would ask, —

" ' What do you want ? '

" They wanted every thing that creature ever wanted, — a pass to go beyond the lines, an order on the Relief Committee for food, protection against a hard landlord, a permit to search for a slave, aid to recover a debt, the arbitration of a dispute, payment of a claim against the Government, the restoration of forfeited property, the suppression of a nuisance, employment in some public office, a gift of money, information on points of law, protection against cruel masters. Others came to give information, or to wreak revenge by denouncing a private foe as a public enemy. A few short, sharp, incisive questions, and then the decision, clear as yes or no could make it, and not another word to be said. Every one got an answer, and the answer was generally right. Under the general's cross-questioning all subterfuges and evasions melted away, and the truth stood out clear and unmistakable.

"At eleven o'clock the letters were placed upon his table, to the number of eighty to one hundred. He read each one, and disposed of them by indorsing short sentences upon the back, when they were handed to the clerks to be answered in accordance with the general's notes inscribed upon them. Others were laid aside for further consideration or personal answer. Military business was next in order, after which lunch was served. Then, till dinner at half-past four or five, writing reports and letters filled up the time. From half-past five till dark, he was on horseback, reviewing regiments, visiting posts, &c. Then home to his private office, where he wrote or dictated letters till ten. Dismissing his tired scribes, he finished the day's work by writing his private letters and despatches."

He kept his work up, — never put off till to-morrow what should be done to-day. Letters from persons at home, whose sons or husbands were in his army, and who had ceased to write, were always promptly answered, giving the fullest information that could be obtained. It is a conceded fact, that no man ever commanded an army who took more kindly and watchful interest in his soldiers than Gen. Butler during or since the war.

The first and most obvious duty of Gen. Butler was to hold New Orleans; and he felt confident of his ability to do this with his present force. But he desired to do more, and he did do a great deal more ; and, if the re-enforcements he repeatedly asked for had been furnished, he would have captured Port Hudson and Vicksburg, and opened the Mississippi River, and thus saved the immense loss of life and treasure which was spent in their reduction a year later, after they had been so thoroughly fortified and manned.

He kept numerous small detachments of his army active in various parts of Louisiana, capturing small posts of the enemy, and subduing guerrillas. The achievements of these detachments were of the most daring and brilliant character, but the limits of our work forbid detail.

The gallant repulse of Gen. Breckenridge and the destruction of the ram "Arkansas" at Baton Rouge, on the 5th of August, was one of the most notable victories of the war. It was here that the gallant Gen. Williams fell. This brave man was everywhere in the hottest of the fight until near the end, when, coming to a regiment of Indiana troops which had lost all its field-officers, he took command of it himself, and fell mortally wounded while leading the brave Hoosiers to a charge.

GENERAL BUTLER IS SUPERSEDED.

On the 9th of November the Secretary of War assigned Gen. Banks to the command of the Department of the Gulf, including the State of Texas ; and on the 16th of December Gen. Butler surrendered the command to his successor. Why Gen. Butler was relieved, has never been fully known to himself or the people. Secretary Stanton and President Lincoln assured him that it was not on account of any waning confidence in him as a man of honor, or his ability as a general. A firm conviction rests in the minds of the general, and the friends of the Union, that Secretary Seward procured his recall, to placate the foreign ministers who secretly sympa-

thized with the rebels, and objected to his vigorous
mode of suppressing treason.

That it was a great wrong to Gen. Butler, and a
still greater misfortune to the Union cause, is no
longer a debatable question.   He had captured New
Orleans with fifteen thousand troops, against the
opinion of Gen. McClellan, who said it would require
fifty thousand.   He had held it in spite of the efforts
of Breckenridge, Lovell, and Jeff Thompson to re-
take it, though their forces outnumbered his, probably five to one.   What he did for New Orleans and
Louisiana has already been recorded here, and is a
part of the imperishable history of this country.
The following from his farewell address to the citizens of New Orleans will serve as a brief summary
of his career in that city.   He said, —

"CITIZENS OF NEW ORLEANS, — I speak not in bitterness.
I have no personal animosity.   I found you captured but not
surrendered; conquered but not orderly; relieved from the
presence of an army, but incapable of taking care of yourselves.
I restored order, punished crime, opened commerce, brought
provisions to your starving people, reformed your currency,
and gave you quiet protection such as you had not enjoyed for
many years.

"The enemies of my country, unrepentant and implacable,
I have treated with merited severity.   I hold that rebellion is
treason, and treason persisted in is *death*.   Upon this thesis
have I administered the authority of the United States.   I
have not been too harsh.   I might have smoked you to death
in caverns as were the Covenanters of Scotland by a royal
British general, or roasted you like the people of Algiers were
roasted by the French; your wives and daughters might have
been given over to the ravisher as were the women of Spain in

the Peninsular war, and your property turned over to indiscriminate plunder like that of the Chinese when the English captured their capital; you might have been blown from the mouths of cannons as were the sepoys of Delhi, — and yet kept within the rules of civilized war as practised by the most polished and hypocritical nations of Europe.

"But I have not so done. The worst punishment inflicted, except for crimes punishable by any law, has been banishment with labor. It is true, I have lived upon the wealthy rebels, and paid out nearly half a million of dollars to feed forty thousand starving people of all nations, assembled here, made so by this war.

"I saw that this rebellion was a war of the aristocrats against the masses, of the rich against the poor; that it was a struggle for the retention of power in the hands of the few against the many; and I found no conclusion to it, save in the subjugation of the few and the disinthralment of the many.

"I therefore felt no hesitation in taking the substance of the rich who caused the war, to feed the poor who suffered by it. And I leave you with the proud consciousness that I carry with me the blessing of the humble and the loyal, in the cottage of the free and the cabin of the slave.

"I have demonstrated that the yellow-fever can be kept from your borders.

"I have given you freedom of the elections greater than you have ever enjoyed before.

"I have caused justice to be administered so impartially that your own advocates have unanimously complimented the judges of my appointment.

"You have seen, therefore, the benefit of the laws and justice of the Government against which you have rebelled. Why, then, will you not all return to that Government, — not with lip-service, but with the heart?

"If you desire to leave to your children the inheritance you received from your fathers, — a stable constitutional government, — if you desire that they shall in the future be a portion of the greatest empire the sun ever shone upon, return to your allegiance.

"There is but one thing that stands between you and the Government, and that is slavery. The institution, cursed of God, which has taken its last refuge here, in his providence will be rooted out, as the tares from the wheat, though the wheat be torn up with it.

"I have given much thought to this subject.

"Months of experience and observation have forced the conclusion that the existence of slavery is incompatible with the safety of either yourselves or the Union. . . .

"I am speaking the farewell words of one who has shown his devotion to his country at the peril of his life and fortune, who in these words can have no interest nor hope, save the good of those whom he addresses; and let me here repeat, with all the solemnity of an appeal to Heaven to bear me witness, that such are the views forced upon me by experience.

"Come, then, to the unconditional support of the Government. Take your own institutions into your own hands; remodel them according to the laws of nations and of God, and thus attain that great prosperity assured to you by geographical position, only a portion of which was heretofore yours."

Gen. Butler's policy and career are completely vindicated by the fact that his successor was compelled to adopt it, after finding his own a complete failure. Gen. Banks soon learned that his efforts at conciliation brought him into contempt with the rebels, who attributed it to cowardice. They hated Butler, but they feared and respected him. Had he been less severe, they would have despised and defied him.

Gen. Butler sailed from New Orleans for home in an unarmed transport, amid the boom of cannon and the shouts of a multitude of citizens and soldiers, who crowded the wharves to see him embark.

At Washington he was treated with every mark of respect by the President and heads of departments, and by the people.   And from that city to his home at Lowell, his journey was interrupted at each important place by ovations such as only great conquerors or great public benefactors receive.   All the leading men of New York City, without regard to party, joined in tendering him a public reception, at which Mayor Opdyke presided, and Gen. Wool and Senator Morgan made speeches full of eulogy to the distinguished guest of the city.   Gen. Butler delivered, on that occasion, a speech of wonderful power, in defence of the Union and in review of his career, which was received with unbounded enthusiasm by the immense crowd of ladies and gentlemen who filled the Academy of Music.

CHAPTER XVI.

GEN. BUTLER TAKES COMMAND OF THE ARMY OF THE
JAMES. — HIS CAREER BEFORE RICHMOND.

GEN. BUTLER arrived from New Orleans on
the 1st of January, 1863. Before he left the
steamer, he received an autograph letter from President Lincoln, asking him to come to Washington as
soon as he had visited his family at Lowell. Having
his wife with him, the general repaired to Washington at once, and called upon the President. He
informed him that he was very desirous of having
enough negro troops recruited to hold the Mississippi
Valley, so as to relieve the white forces then operat-
ing there. Gen. Butler said, "If you will send me
back to New Orleans in command of the Department
of the Gulf, I will recruit all the colored troops you
want." But, after having been relieved of that command without cause, he could not return as a sub-
ordinate. The President replied, "You were not
causelessly recalled from New Orleans, although the
reason for it does not reflect upon your honor as a
man, or ability as an officer." The French minister
had demanded his withdrawal, saying that, if it was

not done, his Government would probably recognize the independence of the Confederate States.

He then asked him if he would be satisfied with the command of Grant's army on the Mississippi. No, he replied; for that would be unjust to Gen. Grant, of whom he had heard only good reports; and, besides, it would create jealousy against him in the army. "Then," said the President, "we shall find a place for you directly. In the mean time, go home, and rest."

During the next few months Gen. Butler was actively but variously employed, under direction of the President; and in June the matter of his taking command of the army of Tennessee was quite extensively discussed, the President thinking him the man to cut the Confederacy in two, by marching through to Savannah, as Gen. Sherman afterwards did. The committee on the conduct of the war sent Hon. Stephen M. Allen to consult Gen. Butler on the subject; but the project was abandoned for the time, because of the threatened invasion of the North by Gen. Lee. The following letter of Hon. Stephen M. Allen to the committee on the conduct of the war describes an interview with Gen. Butler : —

BOSTON, Jan. 20, 1863.

. . . .
But he thinks a glorious thing could be done by taking seventy-five thousand men, which could be spared from the Potomac and Washington (doing nothing there but keeping rebels off), and starting from Fort Monroe, and landing near Charleston, which he thinks could be done sooner than any army could be transported to their aid, and then take Charleston, which could be

done without difficulty, pass up through the highlands of Georgia, where it is healthy, cut the rebels in two latitudinally, and thus establishing a line of communication with our western army.

.   .   .   .

S. M. ALLEN.

In November, 1863, Gen. Butler was ordered to relieve Gen. Foster, and take command of the department of Virginia and North Carolina, with instructions to make preparations for an early spring movement upon Richmond. His first work was to recruit a large number of negro troops; and now, as all the colored troops recruited in the North and in Maryland were sent to him, he soon had quite a large negro force, which he equipped and drilled.

About the 1st of February, 1864, he learned that the Confederate forces had chiefly been withdrawn from Richmond; and he planned an expedition, under Gen. Wistar, to make a raid upon Richmond, with a view to the capture of the Confederate Government. He desired particularly to get Jefferson Davis into his hands, as a prisoner, with a view to asking him to revise a certain proclamation he had made in regard to the general, after his recall from New Orleans.

The expedition failed through the treachery of a Union soldier, who deserted to the rebels, and put them on their guard, thus preventing a surprise at Bottom's Bridge, across the Chickahominy, upon which the whole matter depended.

On the 1st of April, Gen. Grant having been assigned to the command of the armies of the United

States, with headquarters at Washington, visited
Gen. Butler at Fortress Monroe, for the purpose of
conferring with him in regard to a plan for a campaign against Richmond. ·↑ The plan agreed upon at
that conference was substantially as follows ; and it
was Gen. Butler's plan, Gen. Grant seeing the wisdom of it, and adopting it. —

To capture City Point, and the peninsula of Bermuda Hundreds, between the rivers Appomattox,
and James, as a base of operations and supplies
against Richmond. Our navy being superior to that
of the rebels, it could hold both rivers as high up as
Aikin's Landing, eight miles from Richmond. There
was a deep, impassable ravine running nearly half
across the neck of the peninsula toward the Appomattox, which was almost met by another ravine from
this river, having about one mile and a half of high
ground between them, which should be fortified and
made as impregnable as Fortress Monroe, thus securing for the Union army a foothold within eight miles
of the rebel capital, from which it could not be driven.

It was agreed, that, as soon as the roads should be
settled, Gen. Butler should march his army, re-enforced by the Tenth Corps, Gen. Gilmore commanding, by boats up the James River, seize the peninsula
of Bermuda Hundreds, and store supplies and provisions for both his own and Grant's armies, and fortify
according to his plan. It was agreed that the movements should be so timed, that, after landing at Bermuda Hundreds, Gen. Butler should make a demonstration upon Petersburg, as though that were the

object of the expedition; and that within ten days he should deploy the bulk of his army around Richmond, enclosing it by the line of its outer fortifications, the left of the army striking the James River above. That at the same time Gen. Grant, crossing the Rapidan with his army, should march by the right flank, drive Lee's army before him, if possible striking the James River above Richmond, form a junction with Butler, and scoop the capital out of the Confederacy.

Gen. Butler made the most energetic preparations. Transportation sufficient to move thirty thousand troops, with their artillery, horses, and baggage, and provisions for one hundred thousand troops for ninety days, were procured. Preceded by the navy, he was to advance up the river, and seize City Point and Bermuda Hundreds, leave a force sufficient to begin a line of defensive fortifications, and to hold it in case of disaster. With the rest of the army he was to put himself below Richmond, surrounding it from below and above on the south, where Gen. Grant was to meet him in ten days from the sailing of his expedition, if possible, which was to be at the same moment Gen. Grant crossed the Rapidan.

On the 4th of May, Gen. Butler received a telegram from Gen. Grant in regard to his movements; and that night he commenced his, having diverted the attention of the enemy by a demonstration at West Point, at the head of York River, leading them to believe that was the point at which the two armies meant to form a junction, — which ruse succeeded entirely in deceiving the rebel commanders. On the morning of the 5th, Butler's army sailed up the James, preceded by the navy, and at five o'clock arrived at City Point and Bermuda Hundreds, seizing the only two salient points on the river below, and which were afterwards fortified and held as Forts Powhatan and Pocahontas. Ten thousand troops were landed at Bermuda Hundreds, at eight o'clock in the evening, while his negro cavalry, two thousand strong on the Richmond side of the James, were marching across the Chickahominy to join him at Turkey Bend, opposite City Point, while Gen. Kautz, in command of the white division of cavalry, marched from below Norfolk at the same time, with instructions to cut the Weldon Railroad, destroy the bridges, and then join Gen. Butler at City Point, on the Petersburg side of the river. Learning from one of his secret-service men, just returned from Richmond, that there was no considerable force in that city, and being within twelve marching miles of it, he desired to change his plan so far as to send a flying column of ten thousand men to capture the city that night. But his corps commanders opposed it, not one of them being willing to take command of the expedition. Gen. Butler believed then, and still believes, that Richmond could easily have been captured that night; and the only reason he did not take command of the expedition personally was that he could not trust the details of the expedition which he was managing in other hands. Kautz and Cole, with their cavalry, were out in the neighborhood of the enemy, and might require assistance at any moment. He urged the command upon Smith, then upon Gilmore, and finally offered it to his chief engineer Gen. Weitzel; but they each declined in turn, though Weitzel agreed with Gen. Butler that the plan was entirely feasible, and would probably succeed if attempted.

Gen. Butler thinks that army etiquette alone deterred Weitzel from accepting command of the expedition, after it had been declined by his superior officers. On the following day fortifications were commenced on the left bank of the Appomattox, four miles from Petersburg, and also on the right bank of the James. The general then made a demonstration upon Petersburg, and fought the battle of Swift Creek, . with the apparent intention of crossing it to capture the city; but, as soon as he thought his works strong enough to justify it, he moved upon Richmond with his whole force, except two brigades, which were left on the Petersburg and Richmond turnpike, to hold the rear in case of an advance of troops from Petersburg. He drove the outposts of the enemy, and captured his outer line of fortifications, below Fort Darling; and on the 15th of May he was investing Richmond on the south. His left wing was within a mile and a half of the river above the city, and his right rested on the river below. This was his position, when Gen. Sheridan came to his headquarters, and informed him of the battle of the Wilderness, and that Gen. Grant, instead of marching by his right flank to strike the James River above Richmond, and thus form a junction with him, was marching by his left flank toward Cold Harbor, and that Grant's cavalry forces were then at Turkey Bend, awaiting forage and provisions.

Seeing that, owing to the disaster of the battle of the Wilderness, the original plan had to be abandoned, that Grant was going to City Point, and learning that Beauregard was now in Richmond, and that a large number of troops were coming up from North and South Carolina, and evidently having no further business around Richmond, Gen. Butler retired within his lines at Bermuda Hundreds, and proceeded to carry out the other part of his instructions, by making the fortifications complete and strong. Before that was done, however, Beauregard came down with a large force, and made a vigorous attack upon his lines, but was gallantly repulsed. In speaking of this, Gen. Butler says, —

"If I had known Beauregard's force then as I do now, I should have allowed him to come in, and then dealt with him after he got there. But, as it was, we repulsed him, and continued the line of fortifications; and, within ten days more, had a line that was not and could not be carried, if defended by ten thousand men, by any army of the Confederacy."

Meanwhile, finding that Petersburg had been left undefended, Gen. Butler drew out a column of eleven thousand men from the Eighteenth Corps, to attack that place. This force was to march for that purpose on the second day. It was only four miles; but that night an order arrived from Gen. Grant, for all the available forces to be sent at once to West Point, to re-enforce him ; and this column of eleven thousand men were sent forward, in obedience to that order.   Believing his lines defensible by a small, force, against any force the enemy could send against them, Gen. Butler ordered Gen. Kautz, with his cavalry, to go around and assault Petersburg on the south ; and Gen. Gilmore was ordered to assault it on the north side.   Kautz obeyed orders, absolutely riding over the fortifications into the city ; but Gilmore failed to do his part, and returned without making an attack, — the reason for which has not been satisfactorily given.   He professed to have learned that there was a large force in the city ; but it was subsequently ascertained that it was defended only by four companies of old men and boys.   This is the same Gen. Gilmore who declined to march. into Richmond on the 5th of May at the command of Gen. Butler, not because he was afraid to do so, but chiefly, it is supposed, to prevent Gen. Butler, a citizen-general, from achieving that fame which was justly due to him for his wisdom in planning campaigns, and his promptness and energy in executing his plans when not thwarted by insubordination on the part of corps and division commanders, who, because they had been to West Point, thought it an outrage on them to be placed under a man of brains who had not received a military education there.   This was the true reason why Gen. Butler failed to capture Richmond on the night of the 5th of May, 1864.

The battle of Cold Harbor was fought by Gen. Grant, on the 2d and 3d of June; and here over five thousand of the eleven thousand brave men sent to him by Gen. Butler were lost, in killed and wounded. The remnant returned, and reported that Grant was marching to join Butler at City Point, and desired that preparations be made for his crossing the river at Fort Powhatan; which was done.

As soon as the returned army was rested, Gen. Butler sent Gen. Smith and Gen. Hinks, the latter in command of the colored troops, to make another attack upon Petersburg, which attack was ordered to be made at sunrise; but, although the distance to march was only four miles, it was not made until near sunset, yet it was successful; the defences were all carried. But, as night set in, Smith concluded to wait for re-enforcements from Grant's army; and, while waiting for Hancock's corps to re-enforce him, Petersburg was re-enforced by a portion of Lee's army, who marched in on the other side, — on learning which, he held the lines with his forces, leaving the enemy in possession of Petersburg, which had easily been his, had he obeyed the orders of Gen. Butler, and made the attack early in the morning. Indeed, he could have occupied and held it, had he gone in that night, instead of waiting for Hancock. It is a matter of history, that no troops ever got nearer Petersburg, until the final capture, than did the colored troops under Gen. Hinks, and the white soldiers under Gen. Smith, on that occasion.

After the disaster of the mine in front of Petersburg, in which the army of the James had no part, Gen. Butler obtained leave from Gen. Grant to cross the James River at Deep Bottom, on the side next to Richmond, and afterwards to occupy as far up as Aiken's Landing, including Dutch Gap and the fortifications of the enemy near that, which was successfully done; and the ironclads were moved up just below Trent's Beach, but could go no farther, because the Howlett House battery of the rebels commanded Trent's Beach, and because the water was not sufficiently deep to float a vessel of more than seven feet of draft, and the ironclads drew sixteen. Gen. Butler saw that in any further approaches toward Richmond, or attacks on the forts surrounding it, he could have no aid from the navy, unless this obstacle at Trent's Beach could be overcome. The beach is in the shape of a horseshoe, and seven miles around; and at the head the river bends in at Dutch Gap, so as to be only about four hundred and thirty to forty feet across. Under these circumstances, seeing the necessity of the navy getting through there, he took Gen. Grant and the chief engineer of the army with him to Dutch Gap, and, pointing out the situation, suggested that a canal sixty feet wide, and sixteen deep, be cut through to the upper James River. After Gen. Butler had fully explained the matter, both Gen. Grant and his chief engineer approved the project, and Gen. Butler was ordered to proceed with it. He did proceed with the Dutch Gap canal, until it was nearly completed; indeed, but thirty feet remained to be cut, to reach twenty-five feet water, and enable our navy to sail within four miles of Richmond; and over this thirty feet, between two and three feet of water was running. At this point, the officer in charge of the work was informed that the naval commander did not consider his force strong enough to hold the river against the rebel gunboats. Thus, while Gen. Butler was vigorously opening a channel, through which he might sail to the attack of the rebel fleet, this brave commodore got frightened out of his top-boots at the possibility that the rebels might take it into their heads to avail themselves of this opening to get at him. Gen. Butler says, "I was opening the door, to let the dog get at the wolf; but was ordered to keep it shut, lest the wolf should get at the dog."

This is the secret, and the whole secret, of the failure of the famous Dutch Gap canal project, for which Gen. Butler has received so much criticism from the newspapers, against which he could not defend himself, had he been disposed to do so, without a violation of army etiquette.

Subsequently the rebel vessels did come down, and chase Commodore —— as far as City Point; and could have captured him, and Grant's head-quarters, had they known their strength and the cowardice of this naval poltroon. One of the rebel gunboats got aground, and the others, fearing to proceed without it, stopped to help it off; which circumstance saved the capture of Grant's headquarters and base of supplies at City Point, cutting our army in two, and holding command of the river.

The aforesaid naval commander need not be mentioned here by name. He was subsequently court-martialed, Commodore Farragut presiding, on the charge of cowardice in connection with this expedition ; and the court found him guilty. Let his name sink into oblivion.

Some time in the latter part of August, Gen. Grant sent two expeditions, under command of two of his corps commanders, across the James River, for the purpose of carrying the enemy's fortifications at Newmarket Heights, and getting possession of the outer line of works that protected Richmond. Both expeditions were unsuccessful.

In September, Gen. Butler asked permission of Gen. Grant, to organize an expedition with two corps of white and colored troops, to cross the James River at Deep Bottom, and one, the colored division and a part of the Tenth Corps, to make an attack on the fortifications at Newmarket Heights, and the other to make an attack on Fort Harrison, a short distance above Dutch Gap, on the Varina turnpike, being the salient point of the whole line of fortifications of Richmond along the river, and a very strong work. On the morning of the 29th of September, the colored division, under Gen. Terry, made an attack on Newmarket Heights, and took them after a gallant charge. Then the entire Tenth Corps attacked the fortifications on the Newmarket road. The Eighteenth Corps, under Gen. Ord, crossing at Varina's Landing, on a pontoon-bridge laid for that purpose, made an attack at daybreak on Fort Harrison, cap-

tured it, and, but for the serious wounding of Gen.
Ord, would doubtless have proceeded to Richmond at
once, as Butler's army now had possession of the entire line of fortifications from Fort Harrison around
to the Newmarket road, being the outer line of the
defences of Richmond, and but six miles from the city.
This success so alarmed Gen. Lee, that on the 30th
of September he sent two of his very best divisions
to attack Butler's forces. A severe battle was fought,
resulting in a brilliant victory for the army of the
James. The loss to the rebels was sixteen battle-
flags, and a large number of men, chiefly captured.
It is worthy of mention, that from that day to the
final surrender of Richmond, no troops ever got
nearer the city than did the colored troops of Butler's army on that occasion; and they were the first
to enter the Confederate capital when it was finally
captured.

During the summer of 1864, Gen. Butler not only
had immediate command of the army of the James,
planning and conducting all its campaigns, but he
was also charged by the government with the task of
conducting the exchange of prisoners between the
two belligerent powers, a most laborious duty; and,
besides all this, he had command of the rebel prisoners at Point Lookout.

A personal inspection of Wilmington convinced
Gen. Butler that the blockade there was not effective,
and that it cost a great deal of money to keep it up.
The secretary of the navy was very anxious that
Fort Fisher, which commanded the approaches of the

Cape Fear River, should be captured. Fort Fisher is situated on a sandy promontory running out into the sea, with deep water very close to it. The immense damage done by an explosion of gunpowder at Alnwick, England, in the summer of 1864, suggested to Gen. Butler the possibility of blowing up Fort Fisher by that agent. He wrote to the secretary of the navy, who laid the matter before a board of officers, who approved of Gen. Butler's plan. The experiment was attempted, but failed; and the newspapers very largely laid the blame of the whole matter upon Gen. Butler. But the facts are, that the whole matter was left to the navy, who utterly failed to adopt his plans, or profit by his suggestions. His plan was to put, say, two hundred and fifty tons of gunpowder into a steamer, with fuses of a certain kind, which he procured, running all through the magazine of powder, so as to explode the whole of it at once. The steamer was to be run immediately under the fort, where the explosion would occur in a certain brief period, regulated by clock-work.

He supplied the naval officer having the matter in charge with the proper fuse; but it was not used. The vessel that contained the powder, instead of being run ashore under the walls of the fort, was anchored more than half a mile above it, beside a sandy beach; and, instead of the powder being simultaneously exploded by clock-work, as was planned by Gen. Butler, a fire was simply kindled on the forecastle of the vessel, which, when it burned down to the powder, exploded a small portion of it, and blew the rest into the sea, where, of course, it never burned. Thus it is seen, that although Gen. Butler is entitled to the honor of having suggested a plan for blowing up Fort Fisher, and a plan which doubtless would have succeeded, his plan was not adopted. But Admiral Porter, who had the whole matter in charge, under direction of the Naval Office, and over whom Gen. Butler had no control, adopted a plan of his own, which proved a scandalous failure.

Porter was sanguine of success; and so fearful of the effect of the explosion, that he took his fleet eleven miles away, as a measure of safety. Gen. Butler took his troops down to Fort Fisher; and, after witnessing the bombardment by the fleet, which followed the explosion, and being satisfied that the fort, being practically uninjured, could be taken only by a sacrifice of life too great to be justified under the circumstances, when all that could be gained would be to stop blockade-running, while Sherman was then marching to Savannah, and Fort Fisher and all must soon fall, he, like a brave, humane, and wise commander, resisted the temptation to win fame at the sacrifice of his soldiers, and marched back to City Point.

Prior to this, however, in November, the Secretary of War had sent Gen. Butler to New York City with a portion of his command, with orders to see that no disturbance occurred on presidential-election day. He obeyed this order; and for once, at least, New York enjoyed a quiet and fair election.

After he was relieved from command, Fort Fisher was taken, with a loss of about eight thousand men killed and wounded ; shortly after which, it fell into the hands of Gen. Sherman, just as it would have done, without any loss of blood or life.

The author will close the history of Gen. Butler's military career with the following from Gen. Grant, as given to a correspondent of "The New York Herald," and published in that paper, on the 25th of May, 1878 : —

"As it was, I confronted Lee, and held him and all his hosts far from Richmond and the James ; while I sent, the same day of my advance across the Rapidan, a force by the James River, sufficient, as I thought, to have captured all south of Richmond to Petersburg, and hold it.   I believe now, that if Gen. Butler had had two corps commanders such as I might have selected, had I known the material of the entire army as well as I did afterwards, he would have done so ; and would have threatened Richmond itself, so as materially to have aided me farther north."

CHAPTER XVII.

GEN. BUTLER AS A FINANCIAL REFORMER.

WE have, in former chapters, considered Gen. Butler's career as a lawyer, a politician, a soldier, and an executive officer. We now come to a consideration of his record as a statesman and political economist.

Gen. Butler is a radical conservative, by which is meant that his mind·not only traverses the gamut of ideas, from the basic principles to the ultimate, but possesses the logical power to grasp, hold, and apply the practical deductions of all propositions of truly philosophic character.

He is, therefore, a statesman after the type of Cuvier, Franklin, and Jefferson, the three greatest statesmen and most profound political economists of their time, and all of whom recognized and advocated the fundamental principles of the financial system of which Gen. Butler is the leading representative and most prominent advocate, and which are sustained by the leading financial writers of this country and Europe still, and which were ably set forth by John C. Calhoun and other distinguished foes of the United States Bank.

To write a history of Gen. Butler's career as a financial reformer, is to present the chief events that have culminated in the formation of the national party, and the principles upon which it is founded; for although Thaddeus Stevens, as chairman of the Ways and Means Committee in the House of Representatives in Congress, reported the legal tender greenback bill of 1862, it was Gen. Butler who, in January, 1869, framed the first bill which embodies the principles of a perfect paper money.

The greenback is a government note, a promise to pay, simply a substitute for bank-paper. It is superior to bank-paper in that it rests upon the credit of the nation, instead of depending for its redemption upon a bank corporation: hence it has a uniform value throughout the whole country. It is true that there is no time set when it shall be redeemed, nor any specific provision for its redemption in coin or any other form of money; but the fact that it bears upon its face the promise of the Government of the United States to pay the bearer the amount represented by the bill implies a time when it shall be paid, and furnishes the bullionists an excuse for unsettling the currency and business of the country by constant clamors and efforts for a return to a specie basis and a redemption of the greenback in coin. There is another defect in the greenback, — a defect for which Mr. Stevens was not responsible: it is not a legal tender in the payment of custom dues, or the interest on the public debt, which fact alone has been the cause of the fluctuations in coin, and all

the infamous evils of gold speculations, and the depreciation of our interest-bearing bonds.   The bill above
referred to, which Gen. Butler introduced in the 40th
Congress, January, 1869, authorizes the issuance, by
the Secretary of the Treasury, of treasury certificates,
which shall not be promises to pay, but shall bear
upon their face the denomination or value represented, and a vignette, to prevent counterfeiting;
and, on the back, the law authorizing their issuance.
In all other respects they would be in the similitude
of the greenback.   The law printed upon the back
makes them legal tender money, equal to any money
coined by the authority of the United States.   The
bill provides for the repeal of that part of the national
bank law which authorizes the banks to issue currency, and compels the redemption of all national
bank-notes in these treasury certificates.   It also
provides, that, when the banks surrender their own
notes for treasury certificates, the securities, government bonds, which form the basis of their currency,
shall remain in the United-States treasury, and that
$3\frac{65}{100}$ per cent of the interest accruing thereon shall
be paid to the Government for the use of said treasury certificates.   The bill further provides that any
corporation or individual may deposit the interest-
bearing bonds of the Government with the United-
States Treasurer, or any sub-treasurer, and receive
ninety per cent of the face of said bonds in treasury
certificates, for which they will be charged interest
at the rate of $3\frac{65}{100}$, to be deducted from the interest
accruing on the said bonds so deposited.

On the 12th of January, 1869, Gen. Butler delivered a speech in the House of Representatives of Congress, in support of his said bill. The following are the chief points of that speech : —

He said, —

"We want a *uniform, sound, cheap, stable,* and *elastic* currency.

"All financial writers agree that paper money is the cheapest of any circulating medium. Experience has proven that national bank-notes, based upon the faith and credit of the country, possess the quality of soundness equal to any possible currency; and, as to the elasticity of paper money, there can be no room for argument. Stability is the fixedness of volume of the currency as compared with the property to be measured by it; and no one can doubt that paper money, regulated as to volume by law, is absolutely stable, while money coined of gold or silver, or any other substance, limited in production, and fluctuating as to amount, is unstable and fluctuating.

"Our present paper currency is sound and uniform, and, as to its production, cheap. But, while it costs but little to produce it, it is dear to the people, because monopolized by privileged capitalists: about half of it being fundable into gold-bearing six per cent bonds, which are free from taxation; and the other half issued through banks, which, while they get about eighteen million dollars a year from the Government for issuing the three hundred million dollars for which they pay nothing, they charge the people an average of about ten per cent a year.

"Another fault of our present currency is, that, while it is a legal tender among the people, it is not so in the payment of import dues, or the interest on the public debt, to which fact is due the disastrous fluctuations that have occurred in our mixed system of currency.

"The remedy for this, presented by the hard-money men, is to resume specie payments, that is, return to the system of currency existing before the war; which, if it were not impossible, would be absurd. The first effect of an attempt to reach a specie basis would be a ruinous depreciation of every species of property except government bonds, and of all wages save those of salaried officers, while every bond and note would increase in value to an extent most oppressive and ruinous to the tax-payers and those in debt. Such an unsettling in values the world has never seen, nor any nation endured. It would be equivalent to confiscation by act of Congress of one-third the value of all the property in the country, except bonds and notes. I will not insult the intelligence of the House by any argument upon the feasibility or practicability of this scheme, which proposes to deprive the farmers, manufacturers, merchants, and industrial and enterprising classes, of one-third their values, for the benefit of a few capitalists."

In the light of the fearful experience through which this country has passed since the contraction of the currency began, and especially since the passage of the resumption law, these words of Gen. Butler, uttered ten years ago, become prophetic wisdom of the highest type.

He foresaw then the evils that must attend the financial schemes, which, if not villanous, were insane or idiotic, of those who advocated a return to a coin basis ; and, like a wise statesman, a true friend of the people, he proposed an excellent remedy, in the bill for the establishment of a government paper money, which should be equal to gold in all respects, and free from the limitations and other defects of the old greenback and the national-bank currency.

He says, —

" Let no man say that I desire to establish or perpetuate a depreciated currency. I think I have proposed a currency as valuable as gold, and, for all purposes of a circulating medium,

better than gold; every dollar of which, I doubt not, will soon
be made equal to gold.   But what I do desire is, that the currency shall not be redeemable in gold and silver, so that any
man, because he has a dollar of it, can call for so many grains
of gold, which must be paid him, and the currency cancelled to
that extent; but with his currency he must buy his gold as he
does his wheat, where it can be had in open market.   In other
words, the value of the currency of this country, its volume, its
stability, the values of all property of the country, shall no longer
be at the mercy of the panics, the caprice, the speculations, or
the needs, of the bankers of Europe or the traders of Asia.

"But I hear the bullionists exclaim, 'Our money must be the
same as the money of the world.'   'We cannot have a different
standard of value from other nations.'   I would as soon, or
sooner, have our government, our laws, our institutions, the same
as the institutions of the rest of the world.   We have divested
our government of every trait of the despotisms, every attribute
of the monarchies, and every vestige of the slaveries, of the Old
World, save one; and that is the all-controlling and all-absorb-
ing power by which masses of the people of all nations of the
earth have ever been enslaved, — *coined money*.

"More than three thousand years ago the despots of the
world, as the most potent method to enrich themselves and
their favorites, and perpetuate their tyranny, hit upon the device
of impressing their 'image and superscription,' or other peculiar
stamp, upon pieces of two of the metals, not the most intrinsically useful or the most beautiful, but the most scarce, and difficult of attainment by the masses of the people; thus arbitrarily
making a measure of value and equivalent for which the property of their subjects must be exchanged.   Because of their
capabilities of being so converted into equivalents of power,
the so-called precious metals were eagerly sought after by all
men, in such a degree that they came falsely to be deemed to
have a special intrinsic value in themselves equal to the effigy
of value stamped upon them.

"In the earliest republics, when governments were established by the people for themselves, the worth and potency of

these metals were antagonized as attributes of despotism. They stamped value upon the more common and equally useful metals generally distributed among the people, to be used by them as instruments of exchange and trade.

"Thus, in early Greece, the effigy of the ox, the most valuable of the people's possessions, was impressed upon pieces of brass or iron, intrinsically of little value, but thus made the equivalent of comparatively considerable wealth.

"So Rome, for more than five centuries, used the effigy of the sheep, *pecus*, impressed upon copper for currency, thereby giving the name *pecunia*, by which money and wealth were afterwards designated throughout the world. It is now admitted by all political economists, that finely engraved printing upon paper, fixing its value, is the best of all possible substitutes for coined money for circulation, and cheaper as a currency for a people than gold itself. It may therefore be safely assumed, that, had the arts and education been sufficiently advanced in the Grecian and Roman republics, the money of the people would have been such paper, instead of the ponderous and inconvenient metals.

"Not until the people of these free commonwealths became deteriorated by vices and luxury, yielding their liberties to tyrants either by choice or usurpation, did gold and silver, the ever-ready adjuncts of despotic power in all its forms and degrees, obtain place and scope to do their appropriate and never-failing work, the enslavement of the labor of the masses. It will be remembered, when the victorious Gaul threw his sheathed sword into the scale as the counterpoise of Rome's degradation, the beam was not balanced by her money, but by the ornaments and trinkets of the richer of her citizens; for she had neither gold nor silver coins for more than a century.

"Twelve centuries afterward, when the feudal system divided Europe, just then emerging from the dark ages, into many small principalities and powers, had given petty princes, dukes, barons, and bishops, control of the liberties of the impoverished people, each claimed as his prerogative the right to fix his value to pieces of gold and silver, and the same to change and debase at his will, by which his serfs must measure their possessions, and pay tribute to him of all they had. Coined gold and silver has ever been the handmaid of despotism; the prop of monarchical power; the supporter of thrones; the upholder of nobilities and priesthoods; the engine by which the privileges and pretensions of aristocrats have always been sustained in trampling down the rights, devouring the substance, and absorbing the unrequited labors, of the masses. Through all time the possession of money has given power to the few to enslave the labor of the many for the benefit of princes and nobles; and its use has been the badge of servitude of all peoples of some king or tyrant. To deny this, at one time, was treason.

" Our patriot fathers, founding a government for themselves on this continent, carefully eliminated from its framework every attribute of monarchy and aristocracy, the divine right of kings, patents of nobility, the succession of primogeniture, the law of entail, the fealty of one man to another, — every one of the devices of kingcraft and oppression with which the people are governed by a class, — all, save one: they retained, whether for good or evil, the precious metals stamped with the king's image as the standard by which to measure the property and industry of the new Republic. ' It was a grievous fault,' and grievonsly have their children answered it. Great, wise, and good men, we marvel that they foresaw so much; ' but they saw not all things.'

" It is easy to understand what determined them in this exceptional adoption of gold and silver, which were the monarchical standards of value. They had just emerged from a war for liberty, during which they had seen their paper substitute for that standard rendered quite valueless and useless, because made convertible and redeemable in gold and silver only, where gold and silver were impossible to be had.

" But the Continental currency wanted every thing which could give it value. Issued by an aggregation, or conglomeration rather, of States just struggling for existence, trying an experiment of government in a new world which many of their best people more than doubted would be a failure, and end in anarchy; without checks and guards against over-issues, coarsely engraved, easy of forgery, degraded by counterfeits by their enemies so that it was difficult to distinguish the genuine from the false, — the only wonder is that such a currency was ever capable of the good service it did do in the war of independence."

After a masterly and scholarly review of the history of currency in our own country and Europe, showing that in that period when gold and silver had been the nominal money, paper currency had really been the circulating medium, and that, while coin had been the pretended basis of the paper currency, it had always failed as a redeeming power whenever put to the test, Gen. Butler closed his speech as follows : —

"Instead of this money, the instrument of tyrants, which has wrought all these evils, I propose a paper currency, admittedly the cheapest and most convenient, its value based not only upon the gold in the country, but upon every other source and element of the national prosperity, emancipated from the control of all other nations, whether civilized or barbarous. It is the currency for a free people, strong enough to maintain every other of their institutions against the world, whose governments they have antagonized ; strong enough to sustain the measure of their business transactions with each other, independent of kings, the least, — or bankers, now the most, — potent sovereigns in the world. It is one of the blessings of the war, that we are enabled for the first time to stand alone in our industries and internal commerce, as we have in our institutions.

"It cannot fail to have attracted attention, that the only remedy for all evils brought on by a currency convertible into specie when distress is upon the merchant, ruin upon the manufacturer, and disaster upon the banker, when the banks of the United States, of England, and of France could afford no aid, has always been a suspension of specie payments; i.e., by the use in these, the foremost nations of the world, of an inconvertible paper currency. If such currency is so potent as a remedy for all financial diseases which beset a nation, whether in peace or war, whether arising from over-trading, over-speculation, or over-investment, why may it not be equally beneficial as a fixed, permanent, and staple circulating medium, to supply the demands of business and the necessities of the people?

"The experiment of an inconvertible currency has been tried on the most extended scale, and through long periods of time, and under the most trying circumstances, and has never failed. In 1797, when the British Empire was threatened with rebellion in Ireland, and was sustaining all Europe against the victories of Bonaparte with its subsidies of gold, the question came to her great war-minister, Pitt, Shall the integrity of the empire be lost? Shall France overrun all Europe, and threaten Great Britain in the East? or shall the currency of the empire be the inconvertible note of the Bank of England? He chose the latter, — how wisely, the success of England and the allied armies culminating at Waterloo attest. An inconvertible currency fought the battles of England and of the world from that Sunday morning, the 23d of February, 1797, when the king himself, in council, ordered the suspension of specie payments till the 18th of June, 1815.

"Irredeemable paper laid the foundation of England's manufacturing and commercial prosperity, supplied her navy, which at Trafalgar made her the mistress of the seas, and procured the gold with which all the armies of Europe were paid; and for eighteen years there was neither financial revulsion, business-panic, nor distress. In answer to the objection that it is necessary to have gold currency for foreign trade, I quote Maclaren, — one of the most philosophical as well as accurate writers of England, — in his History of the Currency: —

"'It is remarkable that no difficulty was experienced by our merchants in carrying on their trade with other nations during this period, though they no longer had a stock of bullion kept for them at the bank, by means of which they might adjust their foreign payments. No inconvenience, indeed, of any kind, was felt from the substitution of paper for gold; and, if the bank-directors had so ordered their issues as to keep the mint and market price of gold on an equality, it seems that no objection could have been urged against the paper currency, except its liability to forgery, and we should never have heard of the currency controversy.'

"We remember our own war of the Rebellion, without the legal-tender note, must have come to an end in the beginning of 1862. The banks had suspended, and, like broken reeds the Government could no longer lean upon them. Business was paralyzed, men and supplies could hardly be obtained, the armies were unpaid, and no decisive battle had been fought when Congress passed the legal-tender act of 1862. From that time business received a new impulse, labor was employed, manufactures everywhere sprung up, supplies were abundant; and although by a great error the legal-tender note was not made the money of the Government for all purposes, as it should have been, yet, crippled as it was, it supplied and paid our soldiers, pensioned the wounded, provided for the widow and orphan, and produced a degree of prosperity heretofore unknown, which has been maintained ever since; and during this period of six years financial panics and disasters were unknown and unthought of until the insane attempt of the banker and capitalist to force a return to specie payments by a contraction of the currency.

"During the year 1864 we exported more than one hundred millions of gold and silver, only thirty-five millions of which came from San Francisco, and no one knew the fact from any effect it had on the business of the country. In any other year, while our currency was upon a specie basis, the export of one-tenth part of that sum beyond our production would have produced financial panics, ruin, and distress, greater than that of 1837, when our total export of specie was less than six million dollars.

"Point me to any other six years in the financial history of the country, in which labor has been so well paid; in which production has been so varied and so successful; in which there has not been more than one financial panic, scattering ruin and

disaster through the land. We have heard much of the patriotism of the bankers and capitalists, who are said to have come
forward to lend their gold to the country in its time of utmost
need; but that is exactly what they did not do.

"In December, 1861, the banks suspended specie payments
without right, without authority of law, in violation of their own
plighted faith and promises, so that neither the Government nor
any one else could get a dollar of their gold from their vaults.
When, in pursuance of the act of Congress of 25th February,
1862, $150,000,000 of legal-tender notes were issued, with which
our soldiers were paid, and the debts of the United States cancelled, did the banks or capitalists loan these to the Government, or did we make them for ourselves? On the contrary,
the banks refused even to receive the Government notes on
deposit. When the Government wanted more money to pay
the soldier, and carry on the war, did they get it from the
banker and capitalist? No: they issued their own legal-tender
notes as money, and paid their debts. Having provided that
these notes might be funded into a gold-bearing six per cent
bond, the capitalists bought them up when they fell to a discount of sixty per cent, by selling the gold at that premium,
which they had hoarded in their vaults, and had refused to loan
to the Government, and funded this, which they now call failed
paper, in bonds for the payment of which in gold, or, what is its
equivalent, a return to specie payments, they now howl at the
doors of the Capitol, unmindful of the destruction of value, the
starving of the laborer, and the ruin and devastation they may
cause.

"Although this return to specie payment has been agitated
ever since the war, what petition has come up to you from the
people demanding it at your hands? What meetings of the
people have been held to make to you petitions for relief from
grievances in this behalf? Not one, — not one: only resolutions of boards of trade and bankers.

"I stand here, therefore, for inconvertible paper money, the
greenback, which has fought our battles, and saved our country;
which has been held by us as a just equivalent for the blood

of our soldiers, the lives of our sons, the widowhood of our daughters, and the orphanage of their children.

"I stand here for a currency by which the business transactions of forty million people are safely and successfully done; which, founded on the faith, the wealth, and property of the nation, is at once the exemplar and engine of its industry and power, — the money which saved the country in war, and which has given it prosperity and happiness in peace. To it four million men owe their emancipation from slavery; to it labor is indebted for elevation from that thrall of degradation in which it has been enveloped for ages. I stand for that money, therefore, which is by far the better agent and instrument of exchange of an enlightened and free people than gold and silver, — the money alike of the barbarian and the despot."

Gen. Butler has not found it necessary to materially change his views since the delivery of this speech. On the contrary, he has maintained the position on the currency question then assumed; and by tongue and pen, in the halls of Congress, on the lecture-platform, in the chambers of commerce, on the public rostrum, he has done what he could to educate the people on this vital issue, — the most vital issue ever presented to the American people.

In the mean time the public sentiment of the country has been, at first slowly, but now rapidly, coming in favor of his views. On the 26th of February, 1878, in the House of Representatives of Congress, Gen. Butler delivered a speech upon finance, in which he summarizes his doctrines in a manner so terse, comprehensive, and clear, that none can fail to understand him. He said, —

"We want the greenback for our currency, and mean to have it.

" But I do not desire that the greenback currency should be made to serve the country as it has done, — vilified, insulted, depreciated by the act of the Government itself; being refused not only to be received for all debts due the Government, not even paid for all demands due from the Government.

" The ' American system of finance ' which will obtain in the near future, — and I hope at once, — which I desire, is : —

" First, a dollar that shall have at all times a certain fixed and stable value below which it cannot go.

" Second, I demand that that dollar shall be issued by the Government alone, in the exercise of its high prerogative and constitutional power, and that that power shall not be delegated to any corporation or individual, any more than Charles the Second ought to have delegated his prerogative of stamping gold coin for the benefit of his paramours, as a monopoly.

" Third, I want that dollar stamped upon some convenient and cheap material of the least possible intrinsic value, so that neither its wear nor its destruction will be any loss to the Government issuing it.

" Fourth, I also desire the dollar to be made of such material for the purpose that it shall never be exported or desirable to carry out of the country. Framing an American system of finance, I do not propose to adapt it to the wants of any other nation, and especially the Chinese, who are nearly one-quarter of the world.

" Fifth, I desire that the dollar so issued shall never be redeemed. I see no more reason why the unit of measure of value should be redeemed or redeemable, than that the yardstick with which I measure my cloth or the quart with which I measure my milk should be redeemed.

" Sixth, For convenience only, I propose that the dollar so issued shall be quite equal to, or a little better than, the present value of the average gold dollar of the world, not to be changed or changeable, if the gold dollar grows lower in value or grows higher, or to be obliged to conform itself in value in any regard to the dollars of any other nation of the world; keeping itself always stable and fixed, so that, when all the property of the country adjusts itself to it as a measure of value, it shall remain a fixed standard forever. But, if it is ever changed, it shall change equally and alike for the creditor and the debtor; nor as the dollar based upon supposed gold, whose changes always have given the creditor the advantage.

" This would tend to bring to an end in all matters of finance the contest between capital and labor, the rewards of both being brought into the same medium of exchange.

" By this system of finance the unforeseen fluctuations in the volume of the currency; the fall in values of property, not to be provided against by business foresight; the high rate of interest which eats out the very vitals of enterprise; the means of manipulating the currency, by which the banker grows rich, and the business man grows poor; and the fluctuations of real estate, the most valuable and stable of all possessions, now changing like the variations of the barometer as the whirlwind approaches, — will be as much a thing of the past as are the products of hand-spinning and hand-weaving as compared with the textures woven by the power-loom.

" I sketched in this place this system of finance nine years ago. It was not popular then, perhaps because unknown: it is now much more known, and has become the demand of the people. I have received political persecution, and sometimes almost social ostracism, because of these views, ever since. What motive could I then have had, and now have, to advocate them, except the prosperity, power, and glory of my country?

" Because of this advocacy I have been called a demagogue. If a demagogue, why did I advocate then, and still cling to, an unpopular measure? Demagogues seek to ride into power on popular prejudices. On the contrary, the statesman seeks to remedy hurtful errors in the government of his country, and instruct the popular mind in regard to them, regardless of loss or gain, of place or power. By that standard I am ready to have all my acts tried in the candid judgment of all just men."

It is an interesting though disagreeable fact, that the progressive statesman and religious reformer share the same fate in all ages and countries, — that of being misunderstood, misrepresented, maligned, and persecuted by those in power and position. As illustrations the author points to Garrison, Phillips, Giddings, Hale, Sumner, and Lincoln. The cause for which these labored and suffered has triumphed, hence their persecutions have ceased. They are heroes now, not martyrs ; statesmen, not demagogues. But thirty years ago every one of these men were the subjects of the vilest abuse and bitterest denunciation by the majority of the politicians and editors ; and even the pulpit was in large measure against them. The demagogue floats with the current of popular opinion, merely reflecting the opinions of others, never daring to have one of his own. Thus he avoids arousing the ignorant prejudices of pulpit, press, and party, who join in pronouncing him a statesman.

The true statesman, however, is a different sort of man. He has opinions, and the courage and honesty to express them and defend them. Those who do not agree with him, yet cannot successfully criticise his views, denounce him as a fool or a demagogue. This is the secret of all the ridicule and vile abuse fulminated at Gen. Butler on account of his currency doctrines.

CHAPTER XVIII.

GEN. BUTLER AS A FRIEND OF THE WORKING-CLASSES.

DURING his entire career, public and private, Gen. Butler has shown a keen and active sense of justice. This sentiment is his guide. By it he is governed in his business relations, and to it he is ever true in his political action.

· As a private citizen, an officer in the army, a member of the assembly of his State or of the National Legislature, his influence, his pen, and his voice are active in behalf of those, who, as he justly says, create the wealth of the world by the toil of the hand, and the sweat of the face, but who get but a meagre share of what they create.

In a speech delivered in Congress, May 21, 1878, on his own bill for the relief of the laboring classes, the following eloquent and thrilling sentences occur : —

"Within two years, 1862 and 1864, Congress appropriated sixty-four million dollars to railroad companies, besides giving them, at that time and since, 285,000,000 of acres of the public lands, an empire in extent, and worth, at the price these corporations are charging the emigrants, five dollars per acre, $1,425,-000,000, being, when added to the money subsidies, an amount almost equal to the entire bonded debt of the nation. How much capital received of these vast sums, and how much labor got for its share, can never be accurately known. But one thing is certain: that the industrial classes never got one dollar that they did not work and pay for by their labor. No dividends, no subsidies, no Credit Mobiliers, ever come to labor.

"The laborer is the producer of wealth; capital is the receiver and distributor; and there should be no contest, but an equitable reciprocity between them; neither should get more in fair proportion than the other. As the veins and arteries take up and circulate the blood in the nourishment of the human body, so capital ought to circulate wealth by means of the veins and arteries of trade through the body politic for the nourishment of every part thereof. When the circulation of our blood stagnates, or any organ or member of our body absorbs more than its share, disease ensues, and if a remedy is not applied death follows.

"Is there no stagnation now? Is there no disease in the body politic? and does wealth equally and properly share in just proportion, and nourish all the members of the body of the nation, and circulate equally and steadily through every vein and artery? Or is it stagnant and corrupt around the heart and the head, leaving the arms and feet cold as in death, and the whole body ready to perish? Woe to us if fever sets in, and the paralyzed arm becomes uncontrolled by the will, and strikes home, scattering confusion, riot, and death!

"I speak these words in all soberness and sorrow, because I feel it my duty so to do. I call attention to the wrong, and the necessity of remedy. I call upon Congress here and now to apply that remedy at once. We have spent more than a week over a political question which for its utmost can have no significance in affecting the business of the country, being only whether A or B shall distribute the Federal offices. Would that that week could have been devoted to steady, careful examination of the dangers which sorround us, and an endeavor to apply a remedy!

"Mark my words, for I desire to be held responsible for

them: there is great danger if we allow ourselves to go home, and give no relief to the present condition of the country. When the day of reckoning comes, as come it must, how mean and piti-ful will our economies in appropriations appear!

"I know that these views and the consideration of this sub-ject is not a pleasant one. I neither ask for, hope, nor expect applause for presenting them to this House. If I desired that, I would make a speech, if I could, showing how the value of a United States bond in the hand of a foreign banker could be raised ten per cent; or how it were possible that a favorite claim of some section of the country could be saddled on the treasury; or how the favorite interest of some portion of the country could be subserved by a law adapted to its special inter-ests. Or, if I desired to 'bring down the house' in a storm of applause, I would utter some biting sarcasm upon the intel-lect, or some attack upon the character, of some member of the House.

"For myself, let it not be said I have given no plan or details by which a remedy may be administered."

Strange words these to fall from the lips of a mem-ber of Congress, and harshly they doubtless grated upon the delicate ears of political demagogues of both parties. But they are words of wisdom, born in the brain of a statesman whose love of justice is far greater than his love of party, or office, or power. They reveal a heart that beats responsive to the demand for justice, that in this age, and this country, is being made as never before in any nation.

Gen. Butler is not a sentimentalist. He is not a reformer, in the common acceptance of that term. But he believes in the principles of equity. He has profound respect for right. Did he live in a country ruled by despotic power, he would doubtless be a revolutionist. He would demand a re-organization of the government, on the principles of freedom, equal rights, and justice. But, recognizing the fact that this government is based upon those grand principles, he simply demands that they should become active forces in the body politic, that the statute laws shall conform to the Constitution. This is all that is needed to cure the evils of which the laboring classes complain.

He is not a communist, agrarian, Jacobin, or red republican, but a true democrat. He demands that class legislation shall cease, and all laws be equal in their influence upon all classes, and that all rights under the Constitution shall be maintained and enforced by the legislative, executive, and judiciary powers of the nation. The Constitution makes it the duty of Congress to coin money, and regulate its value, to provide the country with a medium of exchange. Gen. Butler demands that it shall discharge this important duty, and not farm out the job to privileged individuals or corporations. This is the fundamental basis of his currency-reform doctrines. He holds that the public domain belongs to the whole people, and that for Congress to parcel out the public lands to railroad corporations is unjust and vicious legislation.

HE BELIEVES IN UNIVERSAL SUFFRAGE.

Gen. Butler is an uncompromising advocate for universal citizen suffrage, both because that is the palladium of liberty, and because the Constitution guarantees to every citizen of this Republic the right to vote. He was a member of the Judiciary Committee of the Forty-first Congress. His committee was called upon, in the discharge of its duties, to make report upon the subject of the right of the female citizens of the Republic to vote for members of Congress. The committee made two reports : a majority report, written by Mr. Bingham, against the right of woman to the ballot ; and a minority report, presented by Mr. Loughridge, but signed also by Gen. Butler, and the authorship of which is credited to him. That the reader may understand his position on that question, the following extract from that report is quoted here : —

The Constitution is necessarily confined to the statement of general principles. There are regulations necessary to be made as to the qualifications of voters, as to their proper age, their domicile, the length of residence necessary to entitle the citizen to vote in a given State or place. These particulars could not be provided in the Constitution, but are necessarily left to the States ; and this section is thus construed as to be in harmony with itself, and with the expressed objects of the framers of the Constitution, and the principles of free government.

When the majority of the committee can demonstrate that "the people of the States," and one-half the people of the States, are equivalent terms, or that, when the Constitution provides that the representatives shall be elected by the people, its requirements are met by an election in which less than one-half the adult people are allowed to vote, then it will be admitted that this section to some extent sustains them.

The committee say, that, if it had been intended that Congress should prescribe the qualifications of electors, the grant would have given Congress that power specifically. We do not claim that Congress has that power : on the contrary, admit that the

States have it ; but the section of the Constitution *does* prescribe who the electors shall be. That is what we claim — nothing more. They shall be "the people." Their qualifications may be regulated by the States ; but to the claim of the majority of the committee that they may be "qualified" out of existence, we cannot assent.

We are told that the acquiescence by the people, since the adoption of the Constitution, in the denial of political rights to women citizens, and the general understanding that such denial was in conformity with the Constitution, should be taken to settle the construction of that instrument.

Any force this argument may have, it can only apply to the original text, and not to the fourteenth amendment, which is of but recent date.

But, as a general principle, this theory is fallacious. It would stop all political progress ; it would put an end to all original thought, and put the people under that tyranny with which the friends of liberty have always had to contend, — the tyranny of precedent.

From the beginning, our Government has been right in theory, but wrong in practice. The Constitution, had it been carried out in its true spirit, and its principles enforced, would have stricken the chains from every slave in the Republic long since. Yet, for all this, it was but a few years since declared, by the highest judicial tribunal of the Republic, that, according to the "general understanding," the black man in this country had no rights the white man was bound to respect. General understanding and acquiescence is a very unsafe rule by which to try questions of constitutional law, and precedents are not infallible guides toward liberty and the rights of man.

Without any law to authorize it, slavery existed in England, and was sustained and perpetuated by popular opinion, universal custom, and the acquiescence of all departments of the government, as well as by the subjects of its oppression. A few fearless champions of liberty struggled against the universal sentiment, and contended that, by the laws of England slavery could not exist in the kingdom ; and, though for years unable to obtain a hearing in any British court, the Sommersett case was finally tried in the Court of King's Bench in 1771, Lord Mansfield presiding, wherein that great and good man, after a long and patient hearing, declared that no law of England allowed or approved of slavery, and discharged the negro. And it was then judicially declared that no slave could breathe upon the soil of England, although slavery had up to that time existed for centuries, under the then existing laws. The laws were right, but the practice and public opinion were wrong.

It is said by the majority of the committee, that, "if the right of female citizens to suffrage is vested by the Constitution, that right can be established in the courts."

We respectfully submit that, with regard to the competency and qualification of electors for members of this House, the courts have no jurisdiction.

This House is the sole judge of the election, return, and qualification of its own members (Art. V. sect. 5, of the Constitution); and it is for the House alone to decide, upon a contest, who are, and who are not, competent and qualified to vote. The judicial department cannot thus invade the prerogatives of the political department.

And it is therefore perfectly proper, in our opinion, for the House to pass a declaratory resolution, which would be an index to the action of the House, should the question be brought before it by a contest for a seat.

We therefore recommend to the House the adoption of the following resolution : —

Resolved, by the House of Representatives, That the right of suffrage is one of the inalienable rights of citizens of the United States, subject to regulation by the States, through equal and just laws.

That this right is included in the "privileges of citizens of the United States," which are guaranteed by sect. 1 of Art. XIV. of amendments to the Constitution of the United States ; and that women citizens, who are otherwise qualified by the laws of the State where they reside are competent voters for Representatives in Congress.

WM. LOUGHRIDGE.
BENJ. F. BUTLER.

There is no sentimentality in this report. It is simply a legal opinion based upon the Constitution of the United States of America, a deduction which he, as an intelligent and honest member of the Judiciary Committee, could not avoid giving. And the fact that he had the moral heroism to stand by his convictions, against the prejudice of the age, which few public men dare oppose, is proof of his courage, as well as his statesmanship.

CHAPTER XIX.

GEN. BUTLER'S CAMPAIGN FOR GOVERNOR IN 1878.

SINCE the late civil war Gen. Butler has been recognized as a leader of the Republican party; and he has mainly acted with that organization on all matters of national policy except finance.   On the latter subject he has long held views in advance of both the great parties.   In Massachusetts the general has, for years, been forcing certain questions of State reform upon the attention of the people. Unfortunately for the Republican party, it is responsible for the abuses which he desires to abolish : hence those Republican leaders who are benefited by the wrongs to the people, of which Gen. Butler complains, find their selfish interests antagonized by his reformatory propositions.   They therefore oppose any and every movement looking to his election to the governorship.   In 1871 the large majority of the voters of that party desired the nomination of Gen. Butler for governor of the State, but the party managers defeated him in the convention by means known only to party managers.   Col. Russell H. Conwell, in an address before the Aurora Club of Boston in

1874, in speaking of this matter, said, "Gen. Butler saw the State-House lobby so eager for office, that the governor's chair had to be divided and sub-divided, and given to 'commissions,' until Massachusetts had twenty-four governors instead of one, and as many politicians had fat places. He saw they were powerful. At the risk of his nomination he fought them. He saw the newspapers aiding in the work of taxing the people more than ought in justice to be. He needed their influence if office was all he wanted, but he fought them with unsparing hand. He had rather fight monopolies, corrupt office-seekers, and newspapers which could be bought with money, than be governor of the Commonwealth." In 1876 Gen. Butler was nominated for Congress by the Republicans of the Fourth District. The party managers and the newspapers opposed his nomination by all means in their power, fair and foul; but the people were too strong for the rings, and their organs.

Having failed to defeat his nomination, they resolved to prevent his election. The plan adopted was to put Judge E. R. Hoar in opposition to him, with a view to divide the Republican vote, and give the election to the Democratic candidate, Mr. Tarbox. This scheme also failed: Gen. Butler was triumphantly elected to the Forty-fifth Congress by the people, over the opposition of both the Democratic and Republican parties. He has faithfully represented his constituents, the people, without regard to the wishes of the politicians.

That campaign of 1876 marks an era in the history of Massachusetts politics. The nomination of Gen. Butler was a declaration by the people of independence of ring-rule. The campaign which ensued was a war of rebellion against party despotism; and his election, a triumph for the principles of popular sovereignty in the Fourth District.

In the summer of 1878, the people of the State, to the number of 51,700, signed a petition headed by Wendell Phillips, to Gen. Butler, asking him to become an independent candidate for governor of the State, on the issue of "State reform." These petitioners were from all parties, Republican, Democratic, and National, who, without regard to previous condition of party servitude, joined in a movement to emancipate the tax-payers from the despotic, extravagant and corrupt rule of the partisan leeches who had fastened themselves upon the public treasury.

Gen. Butler accepted this popular nomination, in a letter of great ability, but in which he confined himself to the discussion of "State issues."

His nomination was indorsed by the Nationals; and the Democratic party leaders, on assembling in State convention at Worcester, found that a large majority of the delegates coming fresh from the people were in favor of also indorsing the nomination of the champion of reform, Gen. Butler. These leaders protested; but finding themselves unable to control the convention, they seceded from it, and the general's candidacy was unanimously ratified. The seceding faction met some days later in Boston, and put in nomination Judge Abbott. The Republican party nominated Hon. Thomas Talbot; and the Prohibitionists, Rev. Dr. Miner. All knew from the first that either Gen. Butler or Mr. Talbot would be elected. The Abbott party put the judge in the field for the express purpose of aiding the Republican nominee, by dividing the Democratic vote. The Prohibition party, doubtless, acted from conscientious motives, in resolving to stand up and be counted as radical temperance men; but it is probable that the candidacy of Dr. Miner took more votes from Butler than Talbot, for the reason that the general is considered much more sound and firm on the temperance question than Mr. Talbot. This nomination of Gen. Butler for governor was to the whole State, what his nomination for Congress, two years before, had been to the Fourth District. It was a popular uprising of the people against party dictation and ring-rule.

The managers of both the old parties understood this, and became allies at once; and they fought side by side, and shoulder to shoulder, throughout the campaign.

Knowing their weakness, their utter inability to meet Gen. Butler on the true issues before the people, — State reforms, — they resolved to ignore these, and compel a discussion of the great national question of finance instead. They knew he was in advance of the public sentiment of the State on that question; and they shrewdly guessed that it would be impossible for him to educate a majority of the voters, and thus overcome their prejudices in favor of hard money, in one campaign of a few weeks.

Gen. Butler opened the campaign by discussing the State reforms ; but finding the opposition speakers and journals persistent in their determination to ignore these issues, and confine themselves to the basest misrepresentations of his views of national finance, and the vilest personal abuse of his private character and public record, he resolved to discuss the currency question as well as State reform. He made the most able and vigorous canvass of which the annals of American politics contain a record. He delivered about one hundred speeches to immense audiences, in various cities and villages of the State. A few earnest, well-informed speakers supplemented his efforts by sound and vigorous speeches, but it was impossible for him, and his volunteer friends to cover the whole State, or reach a majority of the voters ; but wherever they were heard the people were profoundly impressed with the able arguments presented in favor of a reconstruction of the financial system of the country in the interest of the enterprising and industrial classes of the nation.

But Democratic and Republican hard-money orators literally swarmed over the land, like the locusts and frogs of Egypt. Not only were all politicians of Massachusetts actively engaged in slandering and denouncing Gen. Butler's currency doctrines, but Senator Blaine, Secretary Schurz, Congressman Frye, Col. Ingersoll, and a host of less luminous lights, were imported from other States, to aid in diverting the attention of the people of Massachusetts from the real questions before them, mystify their minds on the true doctrines of finance, and thus roll back the waves of revolution and reform that threatened to ingulf the old parties, and redeem the State.

The author was in this canvass: hence he writes from the standpoint of personal observation. He does not hesitate to say that while Gen. Butler and his friends conducted the campaign, on their part, in a manner worthy American citizens and statesmen, confining themselves to honorable discussion of vital questions; the majority of the opposition speakers and papers resorted to every species of political jug-glery known to the modern demagogue. Still fear-ing defeat at the hands of the people's champion, the Republican party, through its executive committee, issued a circular letter to the clergy of the State, urging them to come to the rescue, and save the party from defeat. Quite a number of the preachers responded by preaching hard-money sermons.

To the old party leaders and their friends, defeat by the people's candidate seemed such a terrible thing, that they resolved to resort to the method known in the South as "bulldozing." Massachusetts justly claims to be an intelligent and cultured State, hence the crude methods of South Carolina were out of place there; but other methods, more refined but no less effective, were available.

"The Boston Herald" gave the anti-Butler men the "cue," in the following editorial which appeared in its issue of Sept. 12, 1878:—

"There will probably be a good deal of 'bulldozing' done in Massachusetts this year, of a civilized type. The laborers employed by Gen. Butler in his various enterprises — mills, quarries, &c. — will be expected to vote for him, or give up their situations. The same rule will hold good on the other side. There will be no shotguns or threats. Every thing will be managed with decorum, adorned by noble sentiments. But the men who oppose Butler employ three-fourths, if not seven-eighths, of the labor of the State. They honestly believe that Butler's election would injure their prosperity. They know that idle hands are waiting to do their work. It is not to be expected that they will look on indifferently, and see their employees vote for a destructive like Butler. Human nature is much the same in Massachusetts and Mississippi. Only methods are different. Brains, capital, and enterprise will tell in any community. It is very improper, of course, to intimidate voters, but THERE IS A WAY OF GIVING ADVICE THAT IS QUITE CONVINCING."

The assumption that the employees of those manufacturing establishments, in which Gen. Butler is a stockholder, would be required to vote for him, was wholly gratuitous, and merely presented for the purpose of an apology for the infamous suggestion which followed. Although Gen. Butler is a patron of manufacturing enterprises, he does not control a single mill in Lowell or anywhere else ; and, if he did, no one who knows him would believe him capable of any unfair attempt to influence the votes of his employees.

In an article commenting upon the above paragraph from "The Boston Herald," "The New York World" says, —

"That paragraph outlined the campaign on the part of the Massachusetts Republicans ; and 'advice' of this 'quiet, convincing' nature was freely given to men whose daily necessities and families to be supported would not allow them to disregard it. Following this declaration a call was issued by Adin Thayer, Chairman of the Republican State Committee, to the manufacturers, inviting them to a secret meeting at the Parker House, Boston, to discuss the subjects connected with the approaching election. The meeting was numerously attended; among others, George F. Hoar being present; and the question of how far manufacturers and employers could safely go in influencing the votes of their employees was considered with much earnestness. It was finally decided, with but few dissenters, that efforts should be made in the direction of influencing the votes of workmen; and the result of this action was made very manifest on election day in the manufacturing towns of Eastern Massachusetts. A few of the men who attended this meeting at the Parker House were disgusted with the spirit of polite bulldozing manifested, and turned their backs upon the whole proceeding. From them the action of the mutiny was subsequently ascertained. This was the beginning, and the plans adopted here and manifested throughout the campaign are believed by many to have effected Gen. Butler's defeat. The usual campaign tricks of shaking hands, &c., were neglected; and, instead of winning men's votes by affected consideration for their families, they were terrorized with hints of the coming winter with no employment. Then a circular, printed cautiously in New York, was sent secretly to all manufacturers who could be reached, as follows : —

"DEAR SIR, — Your co-operation with the Massachusetts Republican State Central Committee is most earnestly requested. It is in your power, by the authority you can exercise over those employed by you, to maintain the honor of Massachusetts, and keep it out of the hands of spoilers and political knaves who have selected Gen. Butler as their candidate. His election would disgrace our State, and ruin our standing at home and abroad. A thorough canvass of those you employ, and an early report to the Secretary of the Republican State Central Committee, will be thankfully received."

That anti-Butler manufacturers, merchants, and bankers compelled their employees to vote for Mr.

Talbot on pain of being discharged, in numerous cases, is a fact well known to many persons in Massachusetts ; and it is established by sworn testimony now in possession of Senator Thurman.

In the light of the facts given here, the election of Mr. Talbot by a small plurality is not a matter for surprise. On the contrary, the fact, that, under all the circumstances, Gen. Butler received the largest number of votes (110,000) ever cast in the State for a defeated candidate, proves the power and establishes the popularity of the man.

Victory often follows fast upon the heels of defeat when the cause one fights for is just. Such is sure to be the result in this case, if Gen. Butler will permit his friends to vote for him for the office of governor this year, 1879.

CHAPTER XX.

CONCLUSION.

JAMES PARTON says of Gen. Butler:—

"He is a great achiever. He is a victorious kind of man. He is that combination of qualities and powers which is most potent in bringing things to pass. He is endowed with a large, healthy, active, educated brain.

"He has courage. He dares to take responsibility. He dares to incur obloquy. He dares to tell the truth.

"He is honest. With opportunities such as no other man has had since the days of Warren Hastings, his hands are spotless.

"He could have made a half-million by a wink; and, if he had done so, he could have come home with a marked reputation for integrity; because then he would have had an interest to create such a reputation, and could not have indulged the noble carelessness with regard to his good name which is the privilege of a man strong in conscious rectitude.

"He is humorous. The pointed humor and vivacity of Gen. Butler's utterances are an element of his success.

"He is a man of faith. He never doubts that the right will triumph.

"He is humane. He was always kindly considerate of the men in his command. He was lenient toward offences resulting from the weakness of human nature. He is generous to the poor. He sympathized with the anxiety of parents who had sons in the army. He is courteous, not to officers and prominent persons only, but to private soldiers, and even the beggar on the street."

Col. Russell H. Conwell, in an address before the Aurora Club of Boston, says of him : —

"Fellow-citizens, I have not attempted to do more in this superficial review than to suggest a few thoughts to lead you in your discussion. But the search which I have made among public documents has been of service to me in explaining many things which seemed dark, and in convincing me that Gen. Butler has greater executive ability, is a braver patriot, a wiser statesman, and a truer friend, than many of us have believed. I am greatly surprised that, notwithstanding the storm of accusation and the thousands of insinuations which almost overwhelm us when we begin an investigation of his public life, — that out of it all there should stand confirmed or proven not one of all these derogatory assertions. That one should suffer himself to be so slandered and misrepresented without more frequent replies, is so strange as to be equalled only by the established fact that the newspapers publish falsehoods about him nearly every day, and the people believe them as often, which have not the slightest foundation in fact or probability. He is a great man ; but a whole army of men as able as he, could not accomplish one-half the evils which rival politicians and their newspapers have laid to his charge. It is a good thing for us to look into these matters, — not in this case only, but in all others like it, — that we may hereafter know whereof we speak, and be able to vote intelligently and without bias in matters of public policy.

"Let me then, candidly and fairly, state to you my conclusions regarding Gen. Butler, with the same freedom with which I intend to speak of other public and representative men of our Commonwealth.

"He is a keen, disciplined lawyer, a shrewd observer of men. He never forgets his friends or his enemies. His battles for himself have sometimes flagged: yet, when he entered the lists as a champion for his friends, he was never known to yield. In behalf of his friends he refuses no weapon placed within his reach, except such as would dishonor his cause. Unselfish in the extreme while his armor is on, he hesitates at no risk, falters not at any sacrifice. Be his enemies or the enemies of his friends who they may, — president, senators, kings, parliaments, legislatures, armies, his own party, the newspapers, or even the churches, — no matter, his foes must succumb. His wars are always on the offensive, and seldom partake of the defensive. The party or the man must be saintly as an angel, strong as Hercules, and as firmly set as the Rock of Gibraltar, to escape the pen or the hand of the artillery of his prolific and wonderful genius.

"As I declared in the beginning, warfare of some kind is his natural element. That passion has made him a great man. That spirit, guided by a powerful, steady brain, has given him the foremost places among the statesmen of this nation and of the world. That desire, coupled with a heart that beats warmly for his comrades, has led him to combat the whole congressional delegation of his State, when by sacrificing a friend to their demand he could himself have ridden triumphant into public favor. That *momentum*, with a desire to see fair play, led him to risk all his own chances for political preferment in the cause of his much-slandered associates. That fearless, chivalric heroism leads him at all times to listen to the millions of applications for assistance, coming from the lowly, to answer which, and to help whom, requires hundreds of letters every day, and a great share of his valuable time. That love of conflict, and the excitement of combat, made him the greatest criminal lawyer of the United States, and naturally led him to the bar as the defender of those who, while under accusation, no matter whether guilty or not, had at the time no friend but him. Lastly, that knightly inborn desire to fight for those who looked upon him for protection has compelled him to provide beautiful homes for his family, and to make provision for companions less fortunate than he, because less hardy and valiant.

"Ah! my friends, I am sure that none of you will accuse me of partisan or illiberal spirit when I say, after mature deliberation, that, when Gen. Butler goes to his grave, there will be more genuine grief in this land than there has been for the death of any statesman since the assassination of Lincoln! Ask the negroes, who first saw the star of freedom through the flashes of his sword, who received the first fire-arms from him, and a brigade of whom were the first troops to enter Richmond! Ask the widows who would have had no bounty! Ask the crippled soldiers and penniless orphans he piloted to clerkships! Ask the unfortunate, ignorant criminals, who would never have been law-breakers had they known friends like him! Ask the merchants of this city, whose homes would have passed under the hammer but for his earnest and freely-given aid! Ask the distinguished members of the Judiciary Committee, the chairmanship of which it is an honor for Massachusetts to hold! Ask our old Commonwealth, who was first and foremost in the war because he offered himself and his all for her good name when he stood all alone! Ask the nation, for whose flag many traitors suffered under his iron hand, and for whose glory and prosperity he has ever fought with unabated zeal against rebels in the field, traitors in Congress, apathy in the Senate, threats from arrogant foreign nations, and the machinations of sneaking, dangerous foes in countless other forms!

"When that time comes, sir, will not some of us regret, — yea, I may say *repent*, — for our supineness in permitting so able a statesman, and so noted a friend of the poor and the weak, to live without our plaudits and encouragement, and fight on in our battles alone?"

In a letter to "The Boston Globe," giving his reasons why he should vote for Gen. Butler for governor, Wendell Phillips said, —

"My friend Mr. Blaine wonders that I and the South should join in this movement, — currency reform. Let me tell him, such movements as this are not of men. Such questions ripen of themselves. It was inevitable, that, after emancipation, this politic-economical issue should present itself. He must not think the bankruptcy of this class, the ambition of that man, the cunning of a party, or the theories of a clique, lifted this question to the surface. As the French courtier said to Louis XVI., 'Sire, this is not a riot, it is a revolution,' so I say to Schurz, Blaine, and Sherman : This is no rotten party falling to pieces, no discontented class clamoring in the dark; this is a step in the ages, a revolution deeper than that which was sealed at Appomattox. It began when Congress declared all men equal : it will never end till it is settled that the people are the source of all power, and safely to be trusted with its exercise over every interest, and in every direction. On one side of the question stand the tory and the coward; those who hate the people, and those who honestly doubt their capacity and discretion. On the other side we see the men who still believe in the Declaration of Independence, and are willing and resolved that this shall be, as Lincoln said, — 'a government of the people, for the people, and by the people.'

"I vote for Gen. Butler because he represents this movement. Ten years ago he had the sagacity to anticipate its appearance, and the patriotism, courage, and magnanimity, to range himself on its side. To-day he is the only prominent political servant of the Commonwealth who accepts it, and throws his influence in its support.

"Men say his advocacy of it is only selfish ambition, seeking to use a popular cry for his own advancement. Ten years ago, when he first gave it his support, it had nothing to offer. The Democratic party, which had held up Jackson's hands in the same battle with banks and money-kings, had forgotten its own record. The Republican party, contented with the flesh-pots of Egypt, frowned on any attempt to curb the power of capital. When Butler committed himself to the plan of a national currency, he seemed to cut himself off from all support; and most men well remember the universal ridicule or howl with which his speech was received. To-day, when this reform is about to seize the helm, he is its rightful representative and leader, who, of all living statesmen, has done the most to honor the Commonwealth by brilliant and efficient service in different capacities.

"Who of our volunteer commanders in the war ranks anywhere near him? His friends have but to name Annapolis, Baltimore, New Orleans, and the 'contraband,' in order to put him in the front rank, if not at the very head, of all volunteer commanders.

"But one service which he rendered the nation in 1861 outdoes, in the view history will take, even all his subsequent well-doing. In 1861, all will remember, there was an hour when it hung doubtful whether the impending war was to be a war of parties, — Democrat against Republican in each State, — or whether it would be the nation putting down a rebellion. Butler, Dix, and a score of such Democrats, by accepting commissions, and flinging their fortunes in with the flag, settled that doubt, and saved the Union. Let no man rashly criticise the patriots who in that dread hour made the scale of the rebel kick the beam.

"In Congress no injustice will be done his Massachusetts associates, and no claim will be made for Butler that any man familiar with Washington will dispute, if one says of him as Lord Clarendon says of Sir Harry Vane, 'Sir Harry Vane was one of the Commissioners, and therefore the others need not be named, *since he was all in any business where others were joined with him.*'

"In spite of all that is alleged against him, I dare affirm that he is, in private life and in his great offices, as upright and honorable as any public servant of the State.

"The political issue which seems ripest to-day for settlement is finance. The man who prophesied, and has done as much as any other to create, this state of affairs, is Gen. Butler.

"The man who has shown the largest capacity to rouse the spirit of the State, and concentrate its strength for any needed purpose, is Gen. Butler.

"The man who, watched by the lynx-eyed malice of a hundred journals, and never shrinking from responsibility in great crises, stands yet as fair in his record as any of his rivals, and far more consistent, is Gen. Butler.

"The man who seems fittest to lead the people in their effort to break the yoke to which Congress has submitted, and which capital now seeks to fasten on the nation itself, is Gen. Butler.

"I shall vote to make him governor of Massachusetts. His success will be the people's triumph."

Hon. Thaddeus Stevens, in a speech in Congress in 1865, said of him : —

"His patriotism, his talents, his acquirements, will hold him aloft amid the attacks of all his enemies. He has rendered services and shown patriotic intention which will make him beloved throughout all this country; and I venture the declaration this day, that if the question could be put to the loyal people, whom they would prefer for the next president, a majority of them would vote for Gen. Butler."

The men whose opinions are quoted here are not only well known to the American people, but they are universally recognized as exceptionally sincere and reliable. They are not politicians. They regard Gen. Butler from the standpoints of the critic, the historian, the reformer.

The public records of the country furnish abundant proof, however, that the military and civil career of Gen. Butler is fully vindicated and amply indorsed by the leading statesmen and generals of this country. The Legislature of Ohio unanimously adopted the following resolution : —

"*Resolved*, That Major-Gen. Butler, by reason of his distinguished services to his country during the present rebellion, is entitled to the most grateful acknowledgment and thanks of the loyal people of the country."

The Legislature of Massachusetts

"*Resolved*, That the thanks of the House are truly tendered to Major-Gen. Benjamin F. Butler for the energy, ability, and success of his administration of the Department of the Gulf."

The following was unanimously adopted by the Congress of the United States : —

"*Resolved*, That the thanks of this House are hereby tendered to Major-Gen. Benjamin F. Butler, for the energetic, able, and humane administration during his command of the Department of the Gulf."

The brief but pointed resolutions quoted have been selected from an abundant stock of similar documents in possession of the author, all showing the high appreciation of the public services of Gen. Butler to the country. Benjamin F. Butler is a man of great and positive character. He leaves the impress of his mind upon whatever he does. He re-organizes public opinion. He establishes precedents. He is a factor in human progress. He makes history. He is one of the colôssal figures of this age, which is destined to stand out in bold relief, while the annals of America shall have a place in the memory of the race.

He is essentially an American. He belongs to the people. His fame rests solely upon the solid basis of personal merit as exhibited in grand achievements, and it reflects credit upon the institutions of the land of his birth.

His fame is world-wide. His words and his actions are discussed in every civilized country on the

globe. He is feared and hated among the aristoc-
racies of Great Britain, of the Continent, and of
Western Asia, as well as of America. He is honored and revered by the liberty-loving people of all
classes throughout the world.

This because he is ever the foremost champion of
the oppressed. He fights on the side of justice, and
under the banners of liberty and equality.